# WOLF BETRAYED

D.N. LEO

# CHAPTER
# ONE

One second.

That was all it took for Killian to make the worst mistake of his life.

When faced with monsters, he couldn't afford to hesitate.

He could have shouted for Ciaran to shoot, since his cousin had plenty of experience in combat--both in business and against supernaturals.

Yet, Killian refrained from ordering a shot--instead giving Ciaran time to process what he was seeing: an illusion of his late wife Juliette.

This pause lasted one second, yet that was enough for the monster to jump at Ciaran.

"I messed up!" Killian groaned.

The cold wind whipped around Killian, biting at his skin as he stood on the rocky mountaintop. The valley below sprawled out before him like a darkened quilt, its shadows shifting and dancing with each gust of wind that made the trees sway. The clouds above hung heavy and gray, threatening to unleash a storm at any moment.

Over and over again, Killian replayed the scene in which Ciaran was taken by the demon.

Ciaran had come to the mountain to help him, and now, he was gone.

Captured.

"Stop blaming yourself," Ivy said softly, her voice almost lost to the howling wind.

She stood next to him, her eyes filled with a mixture of anger and concern. "It won't bring Ciaran back."

"I'm responsible for this."

"No, you're not," she insisted, placing a hand on his forearm. "We'll find him, Killian."

Her touch brought a fleeting moment of comfort, but it wasn't enough to quell the anger bubbling inside him. Killian knew she was trying to calm him, but she was just as angry as he was about Ciaran's capture.

The adrenaline surged through him, urging him to shift into his wolf form, despite knowing that if he did, he would be trapped as a wolf forever due to the curse.

"Control yourself," Ivy warned, her grip tightening on his arm. "Don't let your emotions dictate your actions. Think about the bigger picture, Killian."

It was a struggle to keep his wolf at bay, but Killian knew she was right.

He couldn't afford to lose himself now.

Not when Ciaran needed him. But as much as he tried, he could feel his control slipping.

"Killian," Ivy said urgently, her eyes wide with fear. "Hold on!"

But it was too late. He could feel the shift coming on, and in a desperate attempt to stop him, Ivy tackled him to the ground, her body pinning his as they tumbled onto the cold, hard rocks.

"Stop!" she shouted, shaking him roughly. "You have to stay in control!"

"Get off me!" Killian growled through gritted teeth, his hands gripping her shoulders tightly as he tried to push her away.

"Fight it, Killian!" Ivy pleaded, her face inches from his. "For Ciaran. For us."

Her words pierced through the haze of anger and pain, reaching the core of who Killian was – a protector, a leader, someone who would never give up.

He took a deep breath, forcing the wolf within him to retreat. His body trembled beneath Ivy's weight, but he held on.

Then at the back of his mind, something sparked.

A sensation?

A light?

A thread of energy?

"H - hold on, Ivy. I have an idea ..."

Ivy got off him. "Tell me, Killian."

"Last time my spirit left my body, I could see things others couldn't and move freely through space," he explained, "I can use that knack to track down the monstrous creature and find Ciaran. I think I can sense its stench lingering in the air. It must still be nearby."

"Leaving your body? But wouldn't that leave you vulnerable?" Ivy asked.

"Maybe, but it's our best shot. I can't just jump out of

my own body. You'll have to knock me unconscious, like Ciaran did to me last time. Then stay here to guard my body while I go after the demon in spirit form."

"Are you sure about this?" Ivy hesitated, biting her lip.

"Positive."

"All right," she agreed reluctantly. "But before I do this, promise me you'll come back to me, and get back to your body in once piece."

"Of course, Ivy," Killian murmured, pulling her close.

Their lips met in a fierce, passionate kiss, a reminder of their love and a promise to return. As they broke apart, tears welled in Ivy's eyes.

"Be safe," she whispered, her voice choked with emotion.

"Always," he replied, his gaze steady and unwavering. With one last look of resolve, Ivy raised her hand, striking Killian on the side of his head, knocking him out cold.

As HIS BODY crumpled to the ground, Killian's spirit separated, soaring high above the mountain top. He scanned the valley below, searching for any sign of the demon and Ciaran as the sun began to set behind the mountains, casting long shadows across the rocky landscape.

Killian's spirit soared through the cold air, his senses heightened as he followed the faint scent of the demon.

He marveled at the way the wind felt against him,

the sensation of weightlessness, and the freedom to move without the burden of a physical body. The breath-taking view of the valley below was a stark contrast to the dark purpose that drove him forward.

In the distance, he could see the demon carrying Ciaran on its shoulder like a rag doll, making its way towards an ominous-looking cave.

As Killian drew closer, he realized that the demon appeared completely oblivious to his presence.

This struck him as odd – demons were known for their ability to sense souls and spirits.

Perhaps this thing wasn't a true demon after all, but rather a supernatural creature using a spell to disguise itself.

The cave loomed before him, its entrance shrouded in darkness. Stalactites hung from the ceiling like jagged teeth, ready to devour anyone foolish enough to venture inside. The walls glistened with moisture, and the damp, musty smell of decay filled the air.

Killian shuddered inwardly, steeling himself as he followed the demon into the depths of the cavern.

He watched as the demon locked Ciaran in a small, dimly-lit room, the sound of chains echoing through the chamber.

The room was cramped and oppressive, with water dripping from the ceiling and pooling on the floor.

Ciaran lay unconscious, his once-vibrant eyes now closed and his breathing labored.

As he continued to observe the demon, Killian couldn't shake the suspicion that it wasn't a real demon. The fact that it couldn't see him was one clue, but there was something else – an aura of deceit and trickery that seemed to surround it.

Killian couldn't fight a demon because he wasn't magical. But, if this thing wasn't a demon, then Killian promised himself he would make it pay for this. He'll make sure when he killed it, it would be a slow and painful death.

Killian's spirit hovered in the shadows of the cave, watching as Ciaran slowly stirred from unconsciousness.

The first sign of movement brought a wave of relief through Killian, knowing that his cousin was at least alive. He focused his energy on reaching out to Ciaran, hoping that their blood bond would enable them to communicate.

He had tried that tactic with Ciaran before, and there was no reason it wouldn't work again.

"Can you hear me, Ciaran?" Killian's spirit whispered.

Ciaran's eyes fluttered open, confusion etched across his face as he looked around the room.

"Killian? Where are you?"

"Great, you can hear me. I'm right here with you."

"You're using your spirit travel trick again."

"It's not a trick, because I'll use that to save your ass, so, shut up and listen.

"Okay, shoot ..." Ciaran winced from the pain that coursed through his body. "What's the plan?"

"We need to get you out of here before that demon comes back."

"Sounds great! So, what's the plan? Because I'm sure

if that was a demon that took me, neither you nor I can do magic."

As soon as Ciaran uttered the final syllable, a sinister figure appeared in the doorway. It was a cloaked being with glowing eyes and skin as black as midnight - which seemed to absorb all the faint light in the room.

Instantly, even in spirit form, Killian could feel the cold presence of the creature, eerily circling Ciaran like a panther hungry for its prey.

"Tell me, boy," the demon snarled, its voice dripping with malice. "How did you manage to hit me with that lightning bolt on the mountain? What power do you possess?"

"Shall I hit you again, if only so you can understand the strength behind my blow?"

"Wrong answer," the demon growled, raising its hand.

Dark tendrils of magic swirled around its fingers, and with a flick of its wrist, they lashed out at Ciaran, causing him to cry out in pain.

Killian's spirit seethed with anger, his helplessness only fueling his rage. He desperately wanted to intervene, but he couldn't touch any physical objects, let alone harm the demon.

"You have to stay strong, Ciaran," Killian whispered, his voice strained from the effort of holding back his emotions. "I'll find a way to get you out of this, I promise."

The demon continued its torment, but Ciaran held his ground, refusing to give it the satisfaction of breaking his resolve.

Killian watched as each strike took its toll on his cousin.

"Your suffering is pointless," the demon taunted. "Give me the answers, and perhaps I will spare your life."

"Go back to where you came from. Wait, that's the same as hell. Then should I just say go home?"

"Very well," the demon sneered, raising its hand for another barrage of dark magic.

Killian seethed with so much rage that he phased through the wall into the adjacent cell.

He paced or floated restlessly, racking his brain for a way to help Ciaran.

He glanced at the young girl, about thirteen years old, sitting on the cold stone floor, hugging her knees to her chest. Assuming she couldn't see him, Killian continued to pace, his frustration growing.

"Can you help me?" the girl whispered suddenly, causing Killian to freeze in surprise.

"Y-you can see me?" he stammered, taken aback by her ability.

The girl nodded. "Name's Viv. I'm a psychic, or medium - whatever they call me. The deal is, I see spirits."

"Alright, great, Vivian, I could really use your help."

"It's VIV! And I asked for help first, Wolf Head!"

"Right, Viv. Yes, We can help each other out. I'm Killian."

Killian pointed toward the cell where his cousin remained captive. "There's a demon torturing my cousin, and I can't do anything as a spirit."

Viv snorted. "Not a demon. Just some pathetic scum!"

"What do you mean?"

"The jerk thinks he'll get a ransom out of my family. I mean out of someone's family. Too freaking bad. I don't have a family. He's got nothing, so he locked me in here."

Killian peered at the complex lock on Viv's prison door. "Why do you think it isn't a demon?"

Viv snorted and rolled her eyes. "Demons have real power, not some flimsy veil-like thing. What kind of demon has to resort to locking in a mere druid with some subpar lock spells?"

"So, you're saying you're a druid then?"

"Whatever." Viv sighed. "My point is, this shit-head is probably just a wizard at best."

"It's much stronger than a wizard. You should have seen what Ciaran went through. I get your point though, and agree. I don't think it's an actual magical creature.

"Vivian, do you know how to break the spell that's locking these cells?"

"Maybe." She sat bolt upright. "Let me put it like this: he's so bad, I think he steals his lock spells from other people who actually know real magic. He can barely remember the incantation and has to read it off some crumpled piece of paper. Sure, he may know some shit, but most of what he does is stuff stolen from someone else. He doesn't have any natural talent for this – or anything else, if you get my drift..."

Viv rolled her eyes. "I'm a druid," she said, pointing to her forehead. "I have my third eye, okay? I know where he put the paper - in the hole he calls his bedroom - at the end of the long tunnel, turn left. He uses the same key for everything. So if you get it, you can open this door and your cousin's cell door."

"Thank you." Killian turned around before leaving. "Why can't you read the spell and free yourself if you know all this and can see the paper?"

Viv stared at him, clearly surprised by his question. She had grown up with this fact but never really given it thought.

Killian could sense an overwhelming sadness emanating from her.

Before he could say anything, Viv shrugged. "I don't read. Never gone to school."

Killian chuckled. "Well, I might not be able to read the incantation; it might be in Celtic or some ancient language. And let me tell you, Viv, I didn't do 'much' going to school either. I was made to, but skipped all the time..."

She cracked a smile. "You're a good guy, Woof Head. I can tell. You're as polished as hell – probably speak five languages. And don't go feeling bad about not having a family or anything. That's just my life now; I'm used to it."

Killian nodded solemnly. "I'll go get the key."

"And when you get there, the paper will be folded shut. You'll need to say this phrase: gaelicus verus aperio. That should do it."

"Thanks again," he said gratefully.

With Vivian's guidance, Killian's spirit ventured into the dimly lit chamber, searching every nook and cranny until he found the note hidden beneath a pile of dusty scrolls. He spoke the phrase aloud and with a loud creak, it swung open.

He memorized the spell, the rushed back to Ciaran's cell.

When Killian entered the cell, the demon had left. Ciaran lay still with eyes closed, but Killian detected a faint heartbeat. He was in a critical state; bloodied and bruised yet somehow alive.

"Listen closely, Ciaran," he instructed, his voice barely audible. "I found the spell to unlock the cell. Repeat after me."

"I'll do anything for freedom... and a burger—I'm famished," Ciaran whispered weakly.

Killian recited the spell with precision, his heart pounding as Ciaran echoed each word.

As the final syllable left Ciaran's lips, the cell door creaked open, allowing him to stumble out into the corridor.

"Thank you, Killian." Ciaran steady himself against the wall. "Let's go."

"Hey! Don't you dare forget me!" Viv exclaimed out the tiny window from her prison cell.

"That's Viv, she showed me how to get the lock spell."

"Right, I assume it's the same spell I need to use to open her door?" Ciaran said through gritted teeth, leaning heavily against the wall for support.

As Ciaran staggered towards Vivian's cell, Killian felt a pang of guilt and frustration at his inability to physically help. His spirit form could only watch as Ciaran struggled to make his way forward, each step seeming more painful than the last.

Ciaran began reciting the spell to unlock Vivian's cell, his voice faltering from exhaustion.

As the door creaked open, Vivian rushed out, steadying Ciaran in the process.

"All right, hang in there Pretty Head. Allow me to help you."

"I'll make mincemeat of you," Ciaran warned.

"Don't be so dramatic. Wolf Head can't help you out this time. I'm all you got."

"My name is Ciaran," he murmured.

"Names don't really concern me. You're either a Pretty Head or a Grumpy Brit."

Viv wrapped Ciaran's arm around her shoulders as they made their way towards the cave entrance.

The rocky path was treacherous, especially for the weakened Ciaran, and every step seemed to echo through the caverns, threatening to alert the demon to their escape.

"Almost there," Killian assured them, his spirit flying above them, scanning the surroundings for any sign of danger.

Finally, after what felt like an eternity, the trio emerged from the cave, their lungs filling with the crisp mountain air. They hurried along the hillside, desperate to put as much distance as possible between them and the demon's lair.

"Over here," Killian guided them to a smaller cave, hidden from plain sight by the rugged terrain. "We can hide in here for now."

They heard a roaring flame and a fire ball blast from where the demon's den was.

Viv shrugged. "Well, I have a nasty habit of dabbling with magical fire balls. I couldn't help it when I shared that dingy hell-hole with him - but now I'm out, I can't help myself. The flames won't kill him. But let's just say, we don't have to worry about being hunted by him for a while."

"You're wickedly fearless for a little one, Viv," Ciaran smiled through his pain.

"I'm not so little. You're in bad shape Pretty Head. What should we do?"

"I'll go get Ivy. She can use her healing magic to fix him."

Ciaran, Vivian, and Killian's spirit slipped into the dark recesses of the cave, their breaths shallow as they listened for any signs of pursuit.

The silence hung heavy in the air, only broken by Ciaran's labored breathing and the distant howls of wind that whipped through the mountains.

"Stay right here," Killian instructed.

Ciaran gave a nod and settled onto a rock.

"Be fast, there won't be much time before other demons show up and I'm not sure if I can protect him..." Viv said anxiously.

"Thank you for this," Killian said gratefully. He quickly returned to where he had left Ivy.

# CHAPTER
# TWO

Ivy knelt beside Killian's unconscious body, his pale skin shimmered in the moonlight as it filtered through the trees. Her heart ached at the sight of him, so powerful and strong, yet helpless in the grip of his deadly curse.

A cool breeze rustled through the leaves above, causing Ivy to shiver as she pulled her jacket tighter around her.

She felt so lost, unsure of how to help Killian break free from the curse that plagued him.

"Maybe Nina can help," Ivy murmured to herself.

Desperate for assistance, she reached into her pocket and retrieved her phone. The mountainous terrain made the phone coverage patchy at best, but she had to try.

"Come on, come on," she muttered, willing the call to connect. Finally, she heard the familiar ringtone and exhaled a sigh of relief.

"Killian's down, and I don't know what to do. I need your help."

"Where are you?" Nina's voice crackled through the static.

"Somewhere in the mountains. I'm not exactly sure," Ivy admitted.

"Okay, just stay put. I'll locate your cell signal and find your exact location. In the meantime, I'll alert Killian's pack and bring Damien to you. He might be able to help."

"Thank you, Nina," she said with a worried tone. "But please be careful. There's something else happening here. I can't quite put my finger on it, but it feels like some dark force has been unleashed."

"Understood," Nina replied firmly. "Just hang tight, okay? We'll be there as soon as we can."

As the call ended, Ivy tucked her phone away and glanced back at Killian's still form. She couldn't just sit there and do nothing, so she reached into her bag for her magical tarot cards, hoping they could offer some guidance.

"Please," she whispered as she shuffled the deck, "give me something useful."

She drew a card and flipped it over, her heart sinking as she saw the image before her.

The Five of Swords – a figure holding three swords, two others lying on the ground, and a dark stormy sky in the background.

It was a card that symbolized betrayal, deceit, and conflict. Ivy's thoughts raced as she tried to decipher its meaning. Was someone about to betray them? Would she be forced to choose between those she loved and her own survival?

"Damn it," she muttered, her hands shaking as she clutched the card. The last thing she needed right now was a cryptic message about betrayal.

She needed answers, solutions, not more questions and doubts.

"Killian," she whispered, brushing a strand of hair away from his face. "I won't let you down. I swear."

Ivy stared down at the ominous tarot card, her heart pounding in her chest. The thought of betrayal cut through her like a knife, leaving her feeling cold and vulnerable.

She was no stranger to deception and duplicity, but this time it was different. This time, she had something to lose.

As she grappled with her conflicting emotions, a sudden gust of wind blew through the clearing, sending a shiver down Ivy's spine. Before she could react, a figure materialized before her, ethereal and otherworldly.

"Selene," Ivy breathed, recognizing the goddess instantly.

The divine one standing between good and evil, light and darkness. In a brief encounter with the supernatural, Selene was a mystery to Ivy. She couldn't tell if their meeting was a blessing or a curse.

"Ah, my dear Ivy, it's been far too long since we last spoke. But fear not, I come bearing a message of great importance."

Ivy eyed the goddess. "I don't remember you ever bringing me any good news. Forgive me if I'm skeptical. But I have a hard time believing that you're here to help."

Selene, the alluring goddess of the moon, clicked her

tongue in disapproval.

"It is time," she purred gently yet firmly, her voice as smooth and velvet-like as the night sky. "I sense your turmoil, Ivy. Your loyalty to Killian is admirable, but there are forces at work that you cannot comprehend — forces that threaten not only your love but your very life. Come with me, I'll show you."

"I can't leave him like this. Plus, I don't trust you."

"Very well, my dear. But remember this: the path you walk is treacherous and filled with peril. To survive, you must learn to trust – not just in others, but in yourself as well."

Ivy scoffed, "Thanks for being so vague."

"If you won't join me, I'll bring the vision to you."

"Didn't ask for that either."

"You didn't have to. You will get it when I want you to."

In an instant, Ivy's surroundings shifted. The cold mountain air vanished, replaced by the oppressive heat and sulfuric odor of the Underworld.

She stumbled on the rocky landscape, the weight of Selene's influence heavy in the air around her.

"Where am I?" she gasped, feeling the suffocating darkness closing in.

Ivy's heart pounded in her chest as she realized that Selene had taken her to the depths of Hell itself.

"Behold," Selene murmured, materializing beside her. "Your true heritage awaits."

"What the fuck, Selene. Get me out of here!"

Before Ivy could protest further, a vision unfolded before her eyes.

She beheld an infant, enshrouded in the arms of a hellish deity. His countenance of dread and fascination enthralled her, his deep gaze offering the chance to wield inconceivable authority.

"That baby is you, Ivy. You were born a demon." Selene said, her voice echoing through the infernal caverns. "Blessed with demon magic, destined for greatness. You could rule this realm if you so desired."

Ivy felt sick to her stomach as she watched the demon god perform a dark ritual, imbuing her infant self with the essence of his power.

"However," Selene continued, her voice filled with false sympathy, "the gift bestowed upon you is also a curse. To survive, you must consume the blood of an innocent. The ritual will make you invincible... make you a true goddess of the demons .."

"There is no such thing. You're lying."

Tears welled up in Ivy's eyes as she struggled to comprehend the revelation. She had always known that something had set her apart from others, but never in her wildest dreams did she imagine that she was born of demonic origin.

"You don't have to believe me, but one day the demon king will come for you. He won't say a word, only come to collect his...offspring."

"What do you have to do with this Selene? Lyrisa told me you made me. Did you sleep with the demon king?"

Selene laughed softly. "That servant sure does like to talk. I should have gotten rid of her sooner. Yes, I created you, but I am a goddess after all. Don't confuse my divine creation with earthly consumption. You are merely one of my creations, and you still haven't proven yourself worthy of my efforts."

"So what do you want from me now? Why show me all this now?"

"I'm offering you a way out," Selene smirked. "Sacrifice an innocent soul, and I will help you escape your demonic destiny. In return, I require the chest in the LeBlanc's vault."

Ivy hesitated.

The thought of harming an innocent person tore at her soul, yet the idea of succumbing to her demonic destiny filled her with dread. Her love for Killian only intensified the agony of her decision – could they ever truly be together if she carried such a monstrous secret within her?

"Time is running out," Selene warned, her voice dripping with impatience. "What will it be, Ivy? Will you sacrifice an innocent soul or embrace the demon that lurks inside you?"

"I need to think about this."

"Understood. This is an important decision. But remember, my offer won't last forever."

Ivy closed her eyes and took a deep breath, trying to still the storm of emotions raging within her. She thought of the countless battles she had fought against evil, the relentless pursuit of justice that had defined her life until now.

Could she truly turn her back on all that she believed in? And yet, how could she not seize this chance to rid herself of the darkness that threatened to consume her?

"Time is a luxury you don't have, Ivy. I'll give you a

bit more time to decide. Just remember, every moment you hesitate, the demon within you grows stronger."

With a wave of her hand, Selene returned Ivy to the human world.

The abrupt shift left Ivy disoriented and over-whelmed, her surroundings spinning around her. As she tried to regain her bearings, she realized that Killian would soon awaken from his unconscious state.

Ivy panicked as she noticed the foul stench of demon clinging to her, like a shroud that threatened to suffocate her. She knew Killian's keen senses would detect it, but she had no idea how to cleanse herself of the odor.

"Damn you, Selene," Ivy muttered under her breath, her hands trembling with fear and frustration.

As she stood there, torn between her love for Killian and the monstrous truth of her origins, Ivy vowed to fight her demonic nature with every fiber of her being. But the question remained – how could she save herself without betraying the very ideals that defined her?

AMIDST THE TURMOIL of her thoughts, Ivy caught a small commotion on the other side of the large boulder that loomed over them. Her instincts took over, and she swiftly approached to investigate.

Peeking around the rock, Ivy saw a mother wolf, injured and desperate, attempting to protect her cowering pups from a larger, more menacing wolf. These were normal wolves, not the shifters Ivy was familiar with, but their struggle resonated with her nonetheless.

"Leave them alone!" Ivy shouted.

The larger wolf snarled and bared its teeth, but Ivy's resolve remained steadfast. She grappled with the beast, ignoring the pain in her limbs as it fought back, until finally, she managed to land a fatal blow. The predator collapsed, lifeless, and Ivy stumbled back, panting heavily.

"Go," she whispered to the mother wolf, who hesitated for a moment before nodding gratefully and leading her pups away from the danger.

As Ivy looked down at her hands, she realized they were covered in the dead wolf's blood. A grim idea formed in her mind – perhaps the stench of the blood could mask the demon's scent that clung to her.

"Killian mustn't know... not yet," she muttered to herself, rubbing the blood all over her body.

Just as she finished, a faint moaning sound reached her ears.

Ivy followed the sound to a crevice under a nearby rock, where she found a young pup trembling in fear. Its eyes, full of resentment and anguish, locked onto hers, and Ivy knew instantly that this pup belonged to the wolf she had just killed.

"Hey, little one," Ivy murmured softly, reaching out with a bloodied hand to comfort the pup.

The small creature bared its teeth and bit her hand before darting away, refusing her comfort.

"Guess I can't blame you," Ivy sighed, rubbing her throbbing hand as she watched the pup disappear into the distance.

The weight of her actions and the decisions that awaited her settled heavily upon her shoulders.

"Choose wisely, Ivy," Selene's voice echoed in her mind once more, taunting her with the impossible choices she faced.

With a deep breath, Ivy composed herself before returning to Killian's side. She found him stirring, groaning as consciousness gradually returned to his pale face. His eyes widened in shock when he saw her standing there, covered in blood.

"By the gods, Ivy!" Killian exclaimed. "Are you hurt?"

"No, it's not my blood. I had to protect us from a wolf that was trying to attack."

"Show me." Killian's gaze was intense, probing, as he struggled to his feet.

Ivy hesitated for a moment but decided to take him to the spot where the dead wolf should have been.

As they approached the area, she felt a sinking feeling in her chest. The body was gone.

"Where is it?" Killian asked, his voice tinged with suspicion.

"I ... I don't know. It was right here, I swear."

Killian looked at her, searching her eyes for any sign of deception. Ivy held his gaze, determined not to give anything away about Selene and her dreadful revelation. This was not the time or place to share such a devastating secret.

"Listen, we need to go," Killian said urgently, breaking the heavy silence. "Ciaran's in trouble, he needs your help."

"Of course," Ivy replied, grateful for the distraction.

As they hurried away from the scene, she caught sight of the young pup whose mother she had killed. Its eyes followed them from the shadows among the rocks, filled with a mixture of fear and hatred.

The pup's presence weighed on her conscience like a stone – another reminder of the choices she had made.

And then Selene's voice wormed its way into her thoughts once more, whispering dark temptations.

"Remember, Ivy, the innocent soul you need to save yourself doesn't have to be human. That pup's spirit is still pure, untainted by the world. Kill it now, and you can escape your fate."

Ivy clenched her fists, trying to silence Selene's voice and push away the horrifying suggestion.

She could not, would not, harm an innocent creature – even if it meant saving herself from a terrible destiny. But as the pup's shadow continued to haunt her, she couldn't help but wonder if she would one day regret her decision.

"We need to hurry, Ivy," Killian said, noticing her distraction.

"Right." Ivy swallowed hard, forcing herself to concentrate on the task at hand.

She couldn't afford to dwell on Selene's words or the pup's vengeful gaze – not while her friends were in danger.

It was certain: the Underworld had reached out to her, and there could be no denying it. Her origin was uncovered and she had no way to change it.

# THREE

Killian's heart pounded as he led Ivy through the dense forest, the moon casting eerie shadows on the moss-covered ground. The cave they sought loomed ahead. As they stepped into the cave, Killian noticed the uneven walls and the faint smell of damp earth.

But what he didn't find were Ciaran and Viv.

"Damn it," he muttered under his breath, his frustration mounting.

Ivy's eyes darted around the cave.

"Look at this," she said, pointing to a small mark etched into the stone near the entrance. "I've seen this before - it's from a clan of druids I met once."

"Viv is a druid. Does the sign mean anything to you?"

"Yes, they're safe."

"Are you sure?" Killian asked, his brow furrowed with suspicion. He couldn't shake the feeling that something was amiss.

"Positive," Ivy replied, her voice firm but distant. "We need to keep looking."

As Ivy moved further into the cave, out of Killian's sight, a sudden chill crept down his spine.

He glanced around, searching for the source of his unease when a ghostly figure materialized before him - a spirit of a dead wolf, its once proud form now twisted with pain and sorrow.

"What do you want?" Killian whispered, knowing instinctively that the spirit had a message for him.

The cave faded away, replaced by a vision of Ivy, her eyes cold and merciless, as she plunged a dagger into the heart of the very wolf whose spirit now stood before him. The young pup cried out in the background, its mournful howls echoing through the air as though it knew its mother's fate.

"Monster," a murmur drifted past his ears, invisible voices whispering their accusations. "Ivy is a monster."

"Killian," Ivy's voice broke through the vision, and he blinked in surprise as the scene dissolved, leaving him back in the cave with her. "What's wrong?"

"Nothing," he lied.

He couldn't confront her about the vision, not when they still had to find Ciaran and Viv. But the seed of doubt had been planted, and it gnawed at him relentlessly.

"Let's keep searching," Ivy said, her eyes filled with determination and something else - something hidden behind the veil of her gaze.

Killian nodded, following her deeper into the cave,

but the whispered voices and the accusing stare of the dead wolf haunted him every step of the way.

As Ciaran leaned against the helicopter, Ciaran grimaced in agony as spasms of pain radiated throughout his body. He wondered if any of his bones remained unbroken.

Viv knelt beside him. Her wild eyes darted about as she muttered a string of curses under her breath.

"Damn it, you're too messed up to fly this thing," she snapped, smearing blood from her hands onto her torn jeans. "I could take you to my people. They'd patch you up."

Ciaran shook his head, wincing as the motion caused fresh agony to shoot through him. "No. I trust Killian. He'll find us."

"Fine," Vivian huffed. "But it's not your precious Killian I'm worried about. It's someone close to him. Someone... dark."

She glanced over her shoulder, her gaze fixed on something only she could see.

"Soul reapers are lurking around here, waiting for their chance to snatch you away. They smell death on you, Pretty Head."

Ciaran forced himself to sit up a little straighter, despite the searing pain in his side. "We'll just have to make sure they don't get that chance."

"Whatever," Viv said dismissively, but a flicker of concern crossed her face as she looked at him. "Just promise me you won't die on me while we're waiting, okay?"

"Deal," he replied with a faint smile, then winced again as another wave of pain flowed through him.

"Good," Viv grumbled, shifting to sit against the helicopter herself. "Because if you die, I'm gonna be pissed."

As they sat there, Ciaran found himself watching Viv more closely, seeing the young, rebellious girl beneath the tough exterior.

"Viv, why did you run from your clan?" he asked gently, breaking the silence.

She hesitated for a moment, then sighed. "I didn't want that life. I wanted to be free. So, I ran. But then I got caught by that bastard who wants to be a demon."

"Are you sure he's not divine?" Ciaran asked, curiosity piqued.

"Positive, I told Wolf Head that, and he agreed," she replied with conviction. "The jerk was just a man. A twisted, evil man playing with dark magic."

"Then we'll stop him," Ciaran promised.

Viv looked at him, her eyes widening in surprise. Then she smiled, and it was like the sun breaking through storm clouds.

"Yes, it's unfortunate that my fire wasn't enough to take him out, but we'll find something more powerful and it'll be the end of him.

THE SUN DIPPED below the horizon, casting long shadows across the rugged landscape as Killian's uncle Finn and his men arrived in a flurry of dust and noise.

Nina emerged from one of the vehicles, her face streaked with dirt and worry etched into her features.

"Killian!" she called out, rushing toward him. "Have you found Ciaran?"

"Not yet," Killian replied.

"Let's divide into small groups to search," Finn said gruffly, his men nodding in agreement.

Killian turned to Ivy. "You should go with Nina. We can cover more ground that way."

Ivy hesitated, glancing back at the cave they had just explored. A chill ran down her spine, but she shook it off and nodded.

"All right, let's go, Nina."

The two women ventured further into the rocky terrain, their footsteps echoing off the jagged cliffs.

"Nina..."

"Yes, Ivy."

"Patrick... he was killed by the creature that took Ciaran. I'm so sorry about your dad, Nina."

Nina stopped in her tracks, her eyes brimming with tears.

She clenched her fists, anger and grief warring within her.

"He was never there for us, but... he was still my father." Her voice broke, and she struggled to regain her composure.

"We need to tell Mom tonight."

Ivy nodded solemnly, offering silent support to her adoptive sister.

As they continued their search, Ivy's gaze lingered on the rocks surrounding them. She spotted the young wolf she had killed its mother earlier, its golden eyes fixed on her with an unsettling intensity. Ivy shuddered, trying to focus on the task at hand.

"Hey, what's that?" Nina asked, following Ivy's gaze to the wolf pup. "Why is it watching us?"

Ivy hesitated, unwilling to reveal the details of her encounter with the wolf's mother.

"It's... nothing," she finally said, forcing herself to look away. "Let's just keep searching."

Nina eyed her skeptically but didn't press further.

The two women pressed on, their determination driving them forward as night fell and the temperature dropped.

As they searched, Ivy could feel Killian's suspicion gnawing at her, but she had no choice but to focus on finding Ciaran. She knew that if he remained missing for much longer, the consequences could be dire for everyone involved.

Finally, Ivy and Nina finally stumbled upon Ciaran, leaning against a large boulder, his face was contorted in pain.

Beside him, the wild-eyed thirteen-year-old girl stared at them defiantly.

At the same time, Killian came toward them from another direction.

"Jesus, Ciaran!" Killian exclaimed as he rushed to his

cousin's side, his anger mingling with concern. "We need to get you to a hospital."

Ivy stepped forward.

"No, I can heal him, let me use my healing magic on him."

Killian shook his head, his expression unyielding.

"No. We're taking him to the hospital."

The rejection stung Ivy, and she could feel her chest tighten with hurt and confusion.

"Killian, please," Ivy tried again, her eyes pleading. "I can help him."

"You are not casting any magic on Ciaran if you don't tell me what happened before, Ivy," Killian snapped, glaring at her.

He turned his back on her, focusing on helping Ciaran to his feet.

Ivy watched them, feeling like she'd taken a physical blow.

As they started making their way back, Killian slowed his pace to walk beside Ivy.

She braced herself for his confrontation, knowing it was inevitable.

"Earlier, while you were gone, I saw a spirit," he said, his voice tense. "It showed me a vision of you killing a wolf, and I heard voices calling you a monster. What is that about?"

Ivy's heart raced as panic threatened to overtake her. She couldn't tell him the truth, not now when everything was so uncertain.

"I don't know what you're talking about," she said,

attempting to keep her voice steady. "Maybe it was just your imagination."

"I need you to be honest with me. If there's something going on, I need to know."

"Killian, I swear," she insisted, her gaze unwavering. "I didn't kill any wolf, and I don't know anything about those voices. I'm just worried about Ciaran, that's all."

He nodded. "All right, let's focus on getting Ciaran help. But we'll talk about this later."

As they continued their journey back to the others, the wind picked up, carrying the scent of blood and fear through the night air. She knew that the darkness lurking within her would only grow harder to control.

"I don't want to go to the hospital," Ciaran gritted out, his voice weak but determined. "Take me to the Sanctuary."

"Are you sure?" Killian asked, "You're badly injured, and Ivy's magic—"

"Please, Killian," Ciaran cut him off.

He glanced at the young girl standing nearby, her eyes wide with worry. "And take Viv with us. She needs our help too."

Killian hesitated for a moment, then nodded.

"All right, we'll do it your way. But if anything happens—"

"Nothing will happen," assured Ciaran, though the strain in his voice betrayed his uncertainty.

When they arrived at the Sanctuary, Finn and several others were already waiting for them, their faces a mix of relief and concern upon seeing the battered group.

As they helped Ciaran inside, Vivian trailing behind, Finn caught Killian's arm and pulled him aside.

"Vincent's been asking questions about Adam's death," he whispered, his expression grave. "Word is he's not letting it go, and he's looking for someone to blame."

"Damn it," Killian muttered, running a hand through his hair. "The last thing we need right now is another enemy."

"Maybe we can reason with him," Finn suggested, but the doubt in his voice was clear.

"Who's Vincent?" Ivy questioned, fear rising within her. They had just dispatched Adam, the traitor from Killian's pack. She had predicted revenge would come eventually, but she had never expected it to be so soon.

"He's Adam's younger brother."

"But he's not in your pack?"

"Not all family members are in the same pack, Ivy. Blood ties aren't a choice. But the pack and where your loyalty lies is a conscious decision." He stared intently at her. "Let's focus on getting Ciaran and Vivian settled first. We'll take care of Vincent later."

NINA WRAPPED her arm around Ivy's shoulder, guiding her away from the others and toward the door. The evening air was cold and biting, sharp enough to make Ivy wince as they stepped outside.

"Okay, you need to talk to me," Nina said, finally breaking the oppressive silence. "What happened between you and Killian today?"

Ivy hesitated, uncertain how much she should reveal. She knew that Nina would do anything for her, but there were some things she wasn't ready to share—not yet, at least.

With a deep breath, she began to tell Nina about the wolf, about how she had killed it and the spirit that had appeared to Killian.

"Killian doesn't trust me anymore," Ivy whispered, her heart heavy with pain. "He thinks I'm a monster."

"Hey," Nina said fiercely, pulling Ivy into a tight embrace. "You're not a monster, okay? You're my sister, and I know who you are. Whatever's going on with Killian, we'll figure it out."

The sincerity in Nina's words brought tears to Ivy's eyes, but she couldn't shake the feeling that something darker was happening, something she couldn't yet understand.

Silently, she decided to keep the truth about Selene hidden, fearing what it might mean for her relationship with Killian—and her own survival as a demon.

"Thanks, Nina," Ivy murmured, clinging to her sister for support. "I don't know what I'd do without you."

"Hey, that's what I'm here for," Nina replied, giving her a gentle squeeze before releasing her. "But we've got other things to worry about now. With Dad gone, I have to take care of the mage business, and that means I'll be distracted from making the potion for Killian's Alpha challenge."

"Can someone else help with the potion?" Ivy asked, knowing how vital it was for Killian to regain his full strength for the upcoming challenge.

"Maybe, but I don't want to risk it," Nina said, her brow furrowed with worry. "I need to be the one who makes it, to be sure it's done right. But I can't focus on that if I'm also trying to manage everything else."

"Then we'll figure it out together."

Nina smiled at her, grateful for her support. "All right, let's do this."

They drove to the sprawling metropolis that night. The bright lights of the city illuminated the darkness around them, providing a stark contrast from the serene silence of the Sanctuary they had just left. Ivy was invigorated by the hustle and bustle all around her, allowing her to clear her head and decide what she needed to do next.

# FOUR

The door creaked open, its familiar groan echoing through the dimly lit hallway.

Ivy's heart raced as she and Nina stepped inside, their footsteps muffled by the worn carpet beneath them. The scent of lavender hung in the air, a testament to Fiona's meticulousness when it came to keeping their home clean.

As they entered the living room, they found Fiona perched on the edge of an overstuffed armchair, her eyes wide with anticipation. Her hands were clasped tightly around a steaming mug of tea, though it seemed like she had forgotten about it entirely.

Damien, a wolf that was turned by Killian's blood during a lab session with Nina, bounded over in his furry wolf form. His tail wagged enthusiastically, and a low whine rumbled from his throat as he nuzzled her hand with his wet nose.

"Tell me what's wrong, Ivy," Fiona implored, her

voice laced with concern. "You look like you've seen a ghost."

Ivy hesitated, feeling the weight of Selene's warning pressing down on her chest.

She knew that Fiona was expecting news about Patrick, but there was something off about her adoptive mother, something Ivy couldn't quite place.

She chose not to mention the demon encounter, opting instead to focus on the painful truth that had brought them here.

"Father's is dead," Nina blurted out before Ivy could find the words, her own eyes brimming with unshed tears.

Fiona's hands trembled, causing drops of tea to splash onto her lap. She closed her eyes for a moment, taking a deep breath before opening them again, her expression unreadable.

"How did it happen?" she asked, her voice barely above a whisper.

"An accident in the mountains," Ivy replied, swallowing the lump in her throat. "He didn't suffer."

"Thank goodness for that," Fiona murmured, setting her cup down with a quiet clink. But just as quickly as her sadness had washed over her, Fiona seemed to snap out of it, her attention turning back to Ivy. "But what happened to you up there? You're still shaking."

"Nothing I can't handle," Ivy lied, her voice wavering slightly. She wanted to tell Fiona the truth, but something held her back.

"Still," Fiona insisted, "I want to know what happened."

"Later," Ivy said, forcing a smile, though it felt more like a grimace. "It's not important right now."

"Everything about you is important to me, Ivy," Fiona's words were tender and genuine, which only made Ivy feel guiltier for keeping secrets.

But she couldn't bring herself to reveal the truth just yet.

"Let's just... focus on being together right now," Ivy suggested, her voice thick with emotion.

Nina nodded in agreement, reaching out to give Ivy's hand a reassuring squeeze.

"All right," Fiona conceded, her eyes glistening with unshed tears. "We'll talk later."

As they settled into an uneasy silence, Ivy couldn't shake the feeling that something was amiss.

She watched as Fiona stared at the untouched tea, her mind seemingly miles away.

And even though Ivy knew she had every reason to be preoccupied, she couldn't help but wonder if there was something else her mother was hiding.

***

THE SILENCE in the room grew heavy, pressing down on Ivy like a tangible weight. She glanced at her mother, who was still lost in thought, and then at her sister, whose eyes flickered with concern. Finally, Ivy could take it no longer.

"Mom," she began hesitantly, "I've been meaning to

ask you about something...about my adoption."

Fiona's eyes snapped up to meet Ivy's, her gaze guarded.

"You've always said it was a closed adoption and that you never knew my biological parents."

Fiona swallowed hard, avoiding Ivy's searching gaze.

"That's right, sweetheart. Patrick and I wanted a child, but we didn't think I could bear one, so we decided to adopt. We were told your birth parents wished to remain anonymous."

Ivy clenched her fists, feeling a wave of frustration wash over her.

"But there's more to it, isn't there, Mom? I need the truth. I can't keep living in the dark."

Nina looked from Ivy to Fiona, her brow furrowed in worry. Ivy turned to her sister and, with a trembling voice, apologized.

"Nina, I'm sorry if I never told you. I just assumed you didn't know."

Nina shook her head, a wry smile pulling at her lips. "Honestly, I suspected for a long time. We don't exactly look alike, do we? You're six feet tall, and I'm five foot two."

Ivy let out a small, humorless laugh, grateful for her sister's attempt at levity amidst the tension. But Nina wasn't finished.

"Actually, Ivy..." Nina paused, biting her lip, clearly hesitant to continue. "I didn't just suspect it. I hacked into the adoption system and found out the last name of our biological parents."

"Wait, what?" Ivy stared at her sister in shock, her

heart pounding. "You did what?"

"Please, Nina," Fiona interjected, her voice trembling with desperation. "Don't tell her. It's not right."

"Mom, she deserves to know!" Nina argued, her eyes blazing with conviction.

As Ivy watched the exchange between her mother and sister, she felt a growing sense of unease.

What were they hiding from her? Why was it so important that she didn't know the truth?

The questions swirled in her mind like a storm, threatening to consume her.

"Enough!" Ivy's voice quavered as she struggled to hold back her tears. "I need to know. Please, just tell me."

Fiona squeezed her eyes shut, defeated, while Nina took a deep breath before speaking.

"Your biological mother's last name is Murdoch, Ivy," Nina said softly. "Katrina Murdoch."

The name echoed through Ivy's mind, her emotions a whirlwind of confusion and anger.

If her mother was human, then how could she be a powerful demon as Selene had told her? Nothing made sense anymore, and Ivy felt more lost and alone than ever before.

In that moment, Ivy couldn't help but notice the brief flicker of relief that crossed Fiona's face upon hearing Nina reveal the name.

It was clear there was more to the story, something her mother still wasn't telling her. But for now, Ivy knew she needed to focus on the present and the challenges that lay ahead.

Her past, and the secrets it held, would have to wait.

Before the conversation proceeded further, a sudden scratching at the door interrupted their tense conversation.

The young wolf whose mother Ivy had killed on the mountain appeared, its amber eyes full of fear and desperation.

Damien leaped from his position in the corner of the room and gave chase as the pup darted outside.

"Damien, no!" Ivy shouted, her concern for the pup overriding her anger and confusion.

She sprinted after them, her long legs carrying her quickly through the open doorway and into the night.

Her heart pounded in her chest as she raced after Damien and the young wolf, her mind racing with thoughts of what could happen if she didn't intervene.

The pup had already lost its mother; Ivy refused to let it suffer more pain because of her actions.

"Please, don't hurt it," she silently prayed as she closed in on them, her breaths coming in ragged gasps.

Her emotions swirled like a hurricane within her, threatening to overwhelm her. The weight of her unknown past, the secrets her family kept from her, and now the consequences of her actions all bore down on her as she struggled to hold herself together.

Ivy's heart raced as she rounded the corner, her eyes narrowing on Damien's hulking wolf form.

He had nearly caught the pup, his claws inches away from the young wolf's vulnerable body. In that split second, Ivy didn't hesitate. She surged forward with a burst of speed and struck Damien from behind.

"Leave it alone!" she yelled as her fist connected with

his side.

The force of the blow was greater than she intended, sending Damien sprawling across the pavement with an agonized yelp.

The pup seized its chance to escape, disappearing into the darkness.

Nina arrived just in time to witness the aftermath, her face pale and stricken.

"Damien!" she cried, rushing to his side as he shifted back into human form, pain contorting his features.

"Are you okay?" Nina asked, her voice laced with concern as she tenderly examined Damien's injuries.

"Fine," he gritted out through clenched teeth.

"Come on, let's get you inside," Nina said softly, casting a hurt and accusatory glance at Ivy before helping Damien to his feet. Together, they slowly made their way back toward the house, leaving Ivy standing alone in the cold air.

"Look what you've done," Ivy thought bitterly to herself as she watched them go.

Her anger quickly turned inward, the weight of everything that had happened crashing down on her like a tidal wave. She couldn't help but think of Patrick, the man who had raised her as his own, and how he had prepared her for a life that was becoming increasingly more complicated and dangerous.

Scenes from her childhood flashed through her mind —days spent practicing martial arts under Patrick's watchful eye, nights spent poring over ancient texts, learning spells and arcane knowledge. Despite the grueling training and strict discipline, there had been a sense of security in those days, an anchor that held her steady through every storm.

"Where did I go wrong?" Ivy whispered, as the tears she'd been fighting finally spilled over.

She clenched her fists, trying to hold onto the memory of Patrick's guidance, his unwavering belief in her abilities. But it felt like grasping at smoke, slipping through her fingers and leaving her empty and alone.

Ivy wiped her tear-streaked face with the back of her hand, her heart heavy but determined.

She knew she had to make arrangements for Nina's safety, and there was one person she could count on.

Taking a deep breath, she dialed Nathan's number, the CEO of Light Source, the mage-run private security firm that the Javernick family had relied on for generations.

"Hello?" Nathan's voice came through the line, rich and warm like hot chocolate on a winter evening.

"Hey, Nathan," Ivy said, "I need your help."

"Of course, Ivy. Anything you need," he replied without hesitation.

"Patrick... He's gone. And I need you to take care of Nina for me. Make sure she's safe, whether she wants it or not. Can you do that?"

"Of course, Ivy. I'm so sorry for your loss," Nathan paused, his voice filled with empathy, "We will make sure Nina is safe. You have my word."

"Thank you, Nathan." The relief in Ivy's words was palpable. Knowing that Nina would be protected eased some of the weight from her shoulders.

After hanging up, Ivy closed her eyes and bowed her

head in reverence. She started to chant the mystical incantations of summoning, and a light engulfed her hands like sapphire flames. The air began to vibrate around her as the minor deity Lyrisa emerged from the swirling smoke with a look of concern on her other-worldly features.

"Lyrisa," Ivy began, "I need your help."

"Ask away," Lyrisa replied, her eyes searching Ivy's face for any sign of what she needed.

"Selene demanded a chest from the LeBlanc's vault. Do you know anything about it?"

Lyrisa's expression turned somber, her brow knitting together as she considered the question.

"I am aware of the chest, but I don't know anything more about it - it is Selene's most guarded secret."

"What can you tell me about my connection to the Underworld? You said Selene created me. This doesn't make sense if my biological mother is human."

Lyrisa's face darkened, her youthful beauty suddenly shadowed by the gravity of the situation. "So, they have made connection," she stated gravely.

"No, not yet." Ivy shivered. "But Selene showed me a vision."

The deity sighed and shook her head slowly. "When Selene gets the Underworld directly involved, it's out of my hands now, Ivy. You must be prepared for whatever comes your way."

Lyrisa vanished into thin air, leaving Ivy standing there alone as an ominous chill ran through her veins and a sinking feeling in her stomach filled her with dread.

# FIVE

Ivy drove back to the Sanctuary.

As she sneaked in, her heart pounded in her chest, each beat echoing louder than the last as she scaled the fence that separated her from Ciaran.

The moonlit night cast shadows across the yard, concealing her movements as she climbed onto the roof with practiced ease.

She knew Killian would never approve of this clandestine meeting, but she couldn't stand by and do nothing while Ciaran suffered. Her fingers trembled as she reached for the window latch, a mix of anxiety and determination fueling her actions.

"Come in, Ivy," Ciaran's voice whispered from within, his keen instinct cutting through her hesitation.

Her hands clung to the branches of the apple tree outside the window, as she lifted her head to peer into Ciaran's room.

From this angle she could see his lean body against the white linen sheets. The dim light reflected off his skin like a golden sheen of honey. His body was injured, but there was a fire in his striking gray eyes that told her he would not be easily defeated.

She entered the room.

"Let me heal you," she said softly, an unspoken plea hanging in the air between them.

"Only if you tell me what troubles you," Ciaran replied, his gaze piercing her soul.

Ivy hesitated, torn between her loyalty to Killian and her need to confide in someone. As much as she wanted to trust Killian with everything, she didn't know how he would take her connection to the demon royal.

She swallowed hard, feeling the weight of her secret bearing down on her.

"Promise me you won't tell Killian."

Ciaran nodded, his own pain momentarily forgotten as he focused on Ivy. "If it does more harm than good, then I won't tell him. You have my word."

With a shaky breath, Ivy let the storm inside her break free, pouring out her fears about her possible ties to the demon royal and the rift it could create between her and Killian.

The more she spoke, the more she felt the crushing weight of her secret lessen, if only for a moment.

Ciaran nodded. "The trouble is far more serious than I anticipated. Very well, I won't inform Killian until I have a glimpse of a resolution. My mind is completely fogged at the moment. Now you can heal me with your magical touch. Please. I'm at your command."

She nodded, gathering her magic and funneling it through her fingertips into Ciaran's body.

The healing energy spread through him like wildfire, knitting his wounds back together. But as it did so, it drained the last of his strength, and he slipped into unconsciousness.

Her heart ached with gratitude for his understanding even as fear continued to gnaw at her insides. She knew that the longer she kept this from Killian, the more it would drive a wedge between them. But for now, she had bought herself some time, and perhaps with Ciaran's help, she could find a way to protect both her love for Killian and the truth about her past.

THE ROOM WAS CLOAKED in silence, the only sound being Ciaran's steady breathing as he slept. Ivy watched him for a moment.

And then, without warning, the cabinet door creaked open, and out stepped Vivian.

"Fuckin' hell!" Ivy whispered sharply, her heart racing.

Viv looked at her with a mischievous grin on her face

"Didn't mean to scare ya. I've got this neat trick where I can hide in plain sight. Comes in handy when you're trying to avoid chores."

Ivy shook her head, trying to catch her breath. "What are you doing here, Viv?"

"Overheard your little chat with Ciaran," she replied casually. "Makes sense now, that dark freaking aura I feel around you. Shit, Ivy, you might be connected to the demon royal?"

"Language, Viv," Ivy chided automatically, but her heart was heavy with worry. "Yes, it's a possibility. But I don't know for sure yet, and I need to find out before I tell Killian."

"Ya know," Viv mused, looking thoughtful, "I saw a druid perform a ritual once – expelled a demon's hold on someone. My clan might have somethin' that could help you."

"Really?" Ivy felt a flicker of hope ignite within her. "That would be great... Thank you, Viv."

"Hey, we're family, right?" Viv grinned. "We stay under the same roof." She grinned.

Before Ivy could respond, the sound of footsteps echoed through the hallway outside the room.

Her heart leapt into her throat.

Killian.

Ivy scrambled up onto the windowsill and swung herself out onto the roof, her heart pounding wildly in her chest.

Killian's voice drifted up to the from within the room.

"Viv, what are you doing in here?"

"Damn, you're good," came Vivian's admiring response. "Ivy was in here earlier, healed Ciaran and left. I think you should give her some fuckin' space, though. She's got shit to sort out."

"Enough with the profanity, Viv. You're only thirteen." Killian growled.

"Thirteen point nine."

Ivy pressed her ear against the roof tiles to eavesdrop, trying to slow her breathing. Her mind racing as she considered her next move.

Ivy's heart raced as she heard the door close, leaving her alone on the roof.

She knew it was only a matter of time before Killian would find her, and the anticipation sent shivers down her spine.

Suddenly, she heard a noise from behind her. Ivy turned to see Killian gracefully landing on the rooftop beside her, moving like a big cat stalking its prey. The smell of his masculine scent filled her nostrils, making her feel lightheaded and weak in the knees. She could see him drawing in her scent as if he were starving for it, and the intensity of his gaze made her breath catch in her throat.

"Killian," she whispered, unable to hide the surprise and desire in her voice.

"We agreed to hold off after our intimacy the other night," he said softly, his voice strained with emotion. "We both know you're not a shifter, and I need to mate with one... but damn it, Ivy, I can't stay away from you."

His words echoed her own feelings, and before she could respond, he had closed the distance between them. He grabbed her with a fierce intensity, crushing his lips against hers while he explored her body with his hands.

His kiss was urgent and desperate, like he needed it to survive. She was lost in the sensation of his touch and his taste; they were consumed by the heat of their passion.

Ivy gasped as Killian's mouth left a hot trail of fire along the curve of her neck, her body arching towards him as their clothes became a distance memory. He lifted her, pressing her against the cool tiles, and she wrapped her legs around his waist.

The hard line of his erection pressed into her thigh with an insistent demand that made her ache, but she wanted even more than that.

She bit down on Killian's shoulder with enthusiasm, enjoying the way he shuddered and slid a hand into her hair.

Ivy was brimming over with passion, wild for this man who made love to every part of her, even the hidden places deep within.

Their movements were feverish, like the flames of a raging inferno, driven by the undeniable connection between them.

Every touch, every caress, every moan seemed to carve itself into their very souls, binding them together in ways neither fully understood.

She felt his fingertips trace the curve of her neck and down her spine; each nerve ending seeming to ignite at his touch. The soft susurrus of their breathless whispers rose and fell around them, enwrapped in warmth and desire.

They were two halves of a whole, drawn together by an unbreakable bond that left no room for doubt or hesitation.

The sensation was dizzying, as if they were consumed by the passion that enveloped them. It was as if time stood still, as though nothing else existed except for this moment—this raw, primal moment that fused their hearts and bodies together in an all-consuming blaze.

As their lovemaking reached a crescendo, Ivy's thoughts were filled with the fear of what could happen if her secret was revealed. But in that moment, all she could focus on was the powerful shifter who held her heart captive.

"Killian," she gasped as they clung to each other, their breaths ragged in the aftermath of their passion. "There's something you need to know."

"Tell me," he murmured, pressing his forehead against hers.

"Damien... he shifted back to human form for the first time since you turned him with your blood," she whispered, her voice trembling. "He might need your guidance."

A mix of concern and determination flashed across Killian's face, and he nodded resolutely. "I'll go into the city to help him," he said, gently disentangling himself from Ivy's embrace. "But we'll talk more about us when I return."

"Promise?" she asked, her eyes searching his for reassurance.

"Promise," Killian replied, sealing their pact with one last lingering kiss.

Ivy and Killian made their way down from the roof, their bodies still tingling with the remnants of their passion.

Ivy's heart raced, her mind reeling from the intensity of their connection as well as the uncertainty of what lay ahead for them both.

"Let's go see Damien," Killian said, his voice gruff

with concern as he ushered Ivy toward the car parked nearby.

As they reached the car, a figure appeared in front of them, emerging from the dappled sunlight like a specter.

It was Quinn, Killian's mother, her piercing eyes filled with an unsettling mixture of sadness and resolve.

"Wait," she called out, causing Ivy and Killian to halt in their tracks. "I have something to tell you both, something important."

"Mother, now is not the best time," Killian replied curtly, clearly eager to get to Damien.

"Please," Quinn insisted, addressing Ivy directly. "You need to ask your adoptive mother, Fiona, about the triad. She knows information about what happened to Killian's father that will change everything."

Ivy felt the weight of Quinn's words settle over her like a shroud, her heart pounding in her chest as she glanced at Killian.

He looked stricken, his face pale and his jaw clenched tightly.

"Mother, why would you withhold such information from me?" Killian demanded, his voice shaking with barely contained anger. "Why keep secrets about my own father?"

"Sometimes, some secrets are not meant to be uncovered," Quinn said quietly, her eyes shimmering with unshed tears. "But I can see now that withholding the truth has caused more harm than good."

"Tell me, Mother," Killian urged, his voice breaking. "What do you know?"

"Ask Fiona," Quinn replied, her voice barely more than a whisper. "She's the one who can explain it all."

Ivy felt her heart twisting in sympathy for Killian, but she also sensed that Quinn's revelation was somehow tied to her own mysterious past and the demonic forces that threatened to tear her world apart.

"Okay," Ivy said softly, placing a reassuring hand on Killian's arm. "We'll ask Fiona about the triad. But first, let's go help Damien."

"Let's hope we're not too late," Killian muttered, his eyes dark and stormy as he turned towards the car.

As they climbed into the vehicle, Ivy couldn't shake the feeling that they were being drawn deeper into a tangled web of secrets and lies, one that would test their love and loyalty to its breaking point.

And as the engine roared to life and they sped off towards the city, Ivy knew that the only way out of this darkness was to face the truth – whatever the cost.

# SIX

The jeep's tires screeched against the pavement as Killian navigated the chaotic streets of South Melbourne, Victoria. He gripped the steering wheel tightly, his knuckles turning white under the pressure.

Ivy, sitting in the passenger seat, couldn't help but notice the world around them was going crazy.

On a side street, a disheveled businessman who had climbed onto the roof of a car and was now shouting incoherently at passersby. Another woman further down the street frantically rummaged through a garbage bin, her hands grasping at nonexistent treasures.

The dark supernatural force that hung heavy in the air was wreaking havoc on the human community.

"Dark magic? Or Underworld attack? What do you think, Ivy?"

"Whatever it is, we need to find Nina," Ivy insisted, pulling out her phone to try calling her sister once more. The line rang and rang, but there was no answer. A sinking feeling settled in Ivy's chest as anxiety gnawed at her insides.

As the jeep lurched forward in the stop-and-start traffic, Ivy made a split-second decision.

"I'm going to Nina's place on foot," she announced, unbuckling her seatbelt.

She could feel Killian's worry emanating from him like a physical force, but she couldn't wait any longer. She needed to know her sister was safe.

"Be careful," Killian warned, his voice strained as he watched her swing open the door and step out into the bustling chaos. The moment her feet hit the pavement, Ivy took off running, weaving her way through the frenzied crowd and dodging the erratic traffic.

The tension in the air was palpable as Ivy sprinted past honking cars and panicked pedestrians. Her heart pounded in her ears, drowning out the cacophony of sirens and shouting. With every step, she felt a growing sense of urgency, as if time was slipping through her fingers like sand.

"Come on, come on," Ivy murmured to herself, as if that would make her run faster, her breaths coming in short gasps as she pushed her legs to move faster.

Her mind raced with possibilities of what could have happened to Nina, each thought more horrifying than the last. Fear clawed its way up her throat, threatening to choke her, but she couldn't let it slow her down.

As she neared Nina's townhouse, she took one last desperate glance around at the chaos unfolding all around her.

She knew that whatever was happening, it had to be

connected to the dark force she and Killian sensed — and somehow, she had to find a way to stop it. But first, she needed to make sure her sister was safe.

***

IVY BURST through the front door of Nina's townhouse, leaving it wide open for Killian. The living room looked like a tornado had ripped through it: overturned furniture, broken glass, and scattered belongings littered the floor.

"Where are you?!" Ivy shouted, her voice cracking with fear.

"Here!" Nina called out from down the hall, her voice strained. "I'm in the laundry room! Damien's going insane!"

Ivy followed the sound of Nina's voice and found her sister standing guard at the laundry room door. A steel bar jammed the handle, keeping Damien locked inside. Her hands shook as she gripped the bar, eyes wide with terror but determination burning within them.

"Damien's trying not to hurt me, but he might hurt himself," Nina explained, her words coming out in short gasps. "He's—"

A guttural snarl interrupted Nina as the laundry room door rattled violently.

Ivy's heart clenched at the sound, her instincts screaming at her to protect her sister.

"Killian will be here any second," Ivy assured her,

trying to keep her own fear from seeping into her voice. "Just hold on."

As if summoned by her words, Killian appeared in the doorway, his eyes immediately locking onto the chaotic scene before him. He seemed to understand the situation instantly, his expression hardening with resolve.

"Damien," Killian called out, his voice steady and commanding, cutting through the cacophony of noise.

"Listen to me. You're experiencing an adrenaline spike from your first shift back into human form. This is normal, but you need to calm down."

For a moment, the only sounds were Damien's heavy breathing and the pounding of Ivy's heart. Then, slowly, the thrashing subsided, replaced by a quiet whimpering. Ivy could sense that Killian's words were reaching Damien, helping him regain control over his own body.

"Focus on my voice, Damien," Killian continued, his gaze never leaving the door. "Feel the ground beneath your feet and take deep breaths. You're safe here. We won't let anything happen to you."

Ivy watched as Killian's unwavering presence seemed to work its magic, calming not only Damien but Nina as well. She couldn't help but marvel at the strength and compassion her alpha possessed, even as he struggled with his own curse.

"Thank you, Killian," Ivy whispered, her eyes meeting his for a brief moment before they both turned their attention back to the laundry room door.

The chaos in the house had subsided, but the dark force that had brought them here still hung heavy in the air.

For now, though, they could breathe a small sigh of relief.

With a nod from Killian, Ivy cautiously opened the laundry room door.

Damien stumbled out, his legs weak and shaky beneath him. His eyes were wide with fear, sweat beading on his brow as he clung to the doorframe for support.

"Damien," Nina breathed, relief flooding her voice. "You're okay."

"Sorry," he murmured, avoiding eye contact. "I didn't mean to scare you."

Before anyone could respond, Fiona burst into the house, her arms laden with steel bars.

She had clearly rushed over to help reinforce the laundry door.

As soon as Damien's eyes met Fiona's, however, it was as if a switch had flipped inside him. His adrenaline spiked once more, and his body tensed, ready to lash out.

"Get her out of here!" Killian barked at Ivy, struggling to hold Damien back as he lunged toward Fiona.

The ferocity in Damien's eyes reminded Ivy of Killian's own struggles when his curse threatened to take control. This was something they needed to handle immediately.

"Mom, you have to leave!" Ivy shouted, grabbing Fiona by the arm and pulling her out of the house.

Fiona looked shocked but didn't resist as Ivy ushered her outside and slammed the door shut, leaving Killian and Damien to sort out the situation inside.

"Wha- what's going on?" Fiona stammered, her confusion apparent.

"Whatever is happening out there is affecting Damien," Ivy explained, her voice tense and urgent. "We need to get away from here, now."

"Yeah .... but why did he react to me that way ...?"

"I don't know, Mom, you tell me."

With no time to waste, Ivy led Fiona to the car and helped her inside, quickly starting the engine and speeding away from the house.

As they drove through the streets of South Melbourne, chaos seemed to follow them: cars swerved erratically, pedestrians stumbled and collided, and tempers flared amongst the panicked crowd.

Ivy gripped the steering wheel tightly, focusing on navigating through the bedlam. She could feel Fiona's worried gaze upon her, but she didn't have time to reassure her just yet. They had to get away from whatever dark force was causing this disturbance.

"Is it something I've done?" Fiona asked, her voice barely audible above the din outside.

Ivy shook her head, not quite sure herself what was happening. All she knew was that they had to put as much distance between themselves and the epicenter of the chaos as possible.

As they continued to drive, Ivy couldn't help but feel a growing sense of dread. The streets were filled with fear and panic, and she knew deep down that this was far from over. But for now, all she could do was keep moving, hoping that whatever lay ahead wouldn't be worse than what they'd already faced.

"It might now be you, it might be me, Mom."

"You? Does this have something to do with what happen on the mountain?"

"It's not on the mountain, it's under the ground, I'm afraid."

"What?"

She could see the genuine confusion in her adoptive mother's eyes. "Never mind, Mom."

As they turned a corner, Ivy spotted Lyrisa standing on the sidewalk amidst the chaos, seemingly untouched by the frenzy around her.

The minor deity caught Ivy's eye and urgently mimed casting a spell.

Ivy understood – healing magic was needed.

"Mom," Ivy said determinedly, "I'm going to try something."

She pulled over near the picturesque lake at Albert Park, switching off the engine before turning to face Fiona.

Ivy raised her hand and murmured an incantation, focusing all her energy on her mother.

A warm, golden light emanated from Ivy's hand, enveloping Fiona.

Within moments, her mother seemed to snap out of her trance-like state, clarity returning to her eyes.

"Ivy, we need to go to Patrick's cave," she urged, urgency in her voice.

"All right, let's go." Ivy started up the car again, and as they drove, the pandemonium in the streets began to subside, returning to a semblance of normalcy.

Upon reaching the national park, Ivy led Fiona along

the familiar trail, which wound its way up the mountain. The tranquil beauty of the surroundings belied the urgency and turmoil that had brought them there.

As they walked, memories of Ivy's grueling training sessions with Patrick in the cave flooded her thoughts. While the magical lessons were valuable, they came at the cost of her childhood innocence and the freedom to simply be a child.

"Are you alright?" Fiona asked.

"Fine, just remembering my training here," Ivy replied, offering a small, nostalgic smile. "It was hard, but it made me who I am today."

"Patrick was cruel, but he always wanted the best for you," Fiona said softly.

"That was because he wanted the best person in the family to represent us in the mage community, Mom. It wasn't because he loved me."

"That's true." Fiona nodded.

When they finally reached the cave entrance, Ivy hesitated only a moment before stepping inside. It was as she remembered: dark, damp, and filled with an aura of power.

The chamber was alive with echoes of intense magical tutelage, days and nights filled with Patrick's observant guidance as he instructed her in the practice of enchantment. A faint luminescence of starlight shone through a small crevice in the granite wall, illuminating the cave with its mysterious shine.

"Let's find out what he left behind," Ivy said, her voice filled with resolve.

The air in the cave felt heavy, charged with magic

and memories. Ivy shivered, her breath visible in the cold, damp atmosphere.

Fiona carefully reached inside a box, pulling out a worn photo that had clearly been handled countless times.

"Look at this," she said, her voice trembling as she handed the photograph to Ivy.

In the dim light, Ivy could make out three men standing side by side, their arms around each other's shoulders. One face was immediately recognizable; Patrick, his eyes filled with warmth and camaraderie.

The emotions hit Fiona like a storm, tears beginning to well in her eyes.

"Who are they?" Ivy asked gently, tracing her finger over the image of the two strangers.

"Patrick, Ayden, and Desmond," Fiona replied, wiping away a tear. "They were best friends, inseparable. But when Ayden died, everything changed. Desmond disappeared – people assumed he was dead too, but no one really knew for sure."

"Is this Ayden, when he was alive?" Ivy asked, pointing at a man who closely resembled Killian's late father. She had only met him in his spirit form, which was drastically different from the picture in front of her.

Fiona nodded. "It's Killian's father. Ayden was the strongest of the three because he was a shifter."

"You know the shifters, you know Quinn. So, why telling Nina and I that you hate wolf shifters? What happened between these three men, Mom?"

"When Ayden died, Patrick... he withdrew from everyone," Fiona said, her voice cracking with emotion.

"He left us – me and Nina – and came to live here, in this cave. I think he believed he could find answers here, something to protect us or maybe even bring Ayden back... But all he found was solitude."

Ivy watched as Fiona's gaze settled on the photo once more, lost in memories and pain. Her thoughts raced to Killian and the information Quinn had shared about the curse and his enemies.

Could this be connected? Was there something in this triad of friends that held the key to the truth?

"Mom," Ivy began, trying to choose her words carefully. "Quinn mentioned something about a triad before... Do you know if Ayden, Desmond, and Patrick were involved in anything that could have led to a curse? Or if they had any enemies?"

Fiona looked up, her eyes searching Ivy's face for a moment before turning away.

"I don't know," she said quietly. "They never spoke much about their work, but I always knew it was dangerous. I just... I never imagined it would lead to this."

"Maybe there's something in Patrick's research that can help us," Ivy suggested, glancing around the cave.

"Maybe ..." Fiona agreed, her voice barely more than a whisper.

Before Fiona could answer Ivy's question, a sudden rumbling beneath their feet made them both freeze in place. The ground shook violently, and the cave walls trembled, sending debris tumbling down around them. Ivy instinctively reached out to steady Fiona, her heart pounding with adrenaline.

"Something's coming ..." Ivy shouted over the

cacophony, her eyes scanning the dark corners of the cave. "We need to get out of here!"

With a firm grip on Fiona's arm, Ivy led her mother towards the entrance, stumbling as the ground continued to heave beneath their feet.

As they emerged into the open air, the earthquake seemed to subside, but Ivy knew better than to breathe a sigh of relief just yet.

"Keep moving," she urged Fiona, pushing her further away from the unstable cave.

As they moved deeper into the woods, it became apparent that something was amiss. The animals that usually populated the forest had grown silent, replaced by an eerie stillness that sent a shiver down Ivy's spine. Suddenly, the quiet was broken by a vicious snarl, and Ivy caught sight of wild animals – wolves, bears, even birds of prey – circling them with malevolent intent.

"Mom, stay behind me!" Ivy commanded, stepping protectively in front of Fiona as she began to weave her magic, drawing on her reserves of strength and determination.

It was then that she saw him: the shadowy figure of Patrick standing among the trees, his eyes fixed on Ivy and Fiona.

If he was dead, she reasoned, this must be his spirit – but why would he be attacking them?

Confused but determined, Ivy decided to use the magic she had previously used to yank the wolf spirit out of Killian. She focused her energy and cast it toward the shadow.

The effect was instantaneous. The shadow recoiled

from the force of Ivy's attack, its form wavering and flickering before vanishing altogether.

As it disappeared, the malevolence that had gripped the forest dissipated, leaving Ivy panting and trembling with exertion.

"Mom..." Ivy began, her voice hoarse from strain. "I don't think Patrick's dead."

"Why not?" Fiona asked, her face pale but her eyes burning with curiosity.

"Because I can't yank a spirit out of itself," Ivy explained, still trying to catch her breath. "It was his energy that was controlling the animals – and if I could affect it like that, then he must still be alive."

Fiona stared at Ivy, stunned by the revelation. She opened her mouth to speak, but before she could form any words, a sudden gust of wind whipped through the trees, carrying with it an ominous whisper that seemed to carry a message only Ivy was meant to hear:

"Find him..."

"Find him? Who, exactly, am I supposed to find?" Ivy asked suspiciously out loud.

The words hung in the air, heavy with portent, leaving Ivy and Fiona to grapple with a new mystery – and an even greater sense of urgency to uncover the truth about Patrick and the curse that threatened them all.

# SEVEN

Killian stood in the dimly lit living room of Nina's cozy home, his eyes never leaving Damien as he knelt beside him. The wild desperation etched across Damien's face was palpable, and Killian could feel the heat of his anguish.

"Damien, listen to me," Killian said softly, his words measured and steady. "You're safe now. We're all here for you."

With a strained growl, Damien finally succumbed, shifting back into his wolf form before them.

Killian looked up at Nina, whose eyes were wide with concern.

"He feels like he's not in control of his wolf, Nina," Killian explained. "Staying in this form is his way of keeping us safe."

"Is there anything we can do to help?" Nina asked, her voice barely audible as she stared down at the massive wolf that was now Damien.

"First, he needs to learn how to tame his wolf before

practicing shifting," Killian replied, running a hand through his hair. "I know someone who specializes in taming wolves. I'll take him there."

"Wait, what about us?" Nina protested, glancing at the collection of pets milling around her feet - Simba, her cat; Pixy, Ivy's husky; and Snuggleworth, Ivy's Cavoodle. "We can't just leave them!"

"Fine," Killian conceded, his face etched with frustration. "We'll all go. Just grab what you need, and let's get moving."

Minutes later, they piled into Killian's car, the interior now a cacophony of animal sounds and nervous energy.

With Nina in the passenger seat, Damien sprawled in the back as a gigantic wolf, and the smaller animals nestled between them, Killian steered the vehicle towards Erin's retreat in Gisborne, on the outskirts of Melbourne city.

The car glided silently along the pitch-black roads, and Killian's thoughts raced with trepidation. He was about to confront a past he had tried hard to forget and might unravel secrets he ought not to know.

Yet his worry for Damien's safety, and the burden of responsibility he felt for him, made it impossible for him to ignore it any longer. But at the same time, he knew that trusting Erin was their only option to help him regain control.

"Promise me you'll look after him," Nina whispered, her voice thick with emotion as she glanced back at Damien's massive form.

"Of course," Killian replied, giving her a reassuring smile. "I won't let anything happen to him."

The car pulled up to a charming cottage, nestled amidst lush greenery and towering trees.

Killian couldn't help but admire the serenity of Erin's retreat – a stark contrast to his own tumultuous life. The green siding of the building was dotted with tiny light blue flowers that were almost white.

"Here we are," Killian announced as he killed the engine and glanced at Nina.

She gave him a determined nod, her eyes filled with anxiety for Damien. The animals stirred in the backseat, sensing their arrival.

As they stepped out of the car, the front door of the cottage swung open, revealing Erin.

Moonlight cast an ethereal glow upon her, accentuating her wild beauty. Her wavy auburn hair fell around her shoulders, framing a face that was both fierce and alluring, her green eyes shimmering like emeralds. Killian felt a familiar pull toward her, his heart tightening at the sight of her. It had been years since they last met, yet it felt like no time had passed at all.

"Killian," she greeted warmly, her voice smooth as honey. "It's been too long."

"Erin," he replied, struggling to keep his voice steady. "Thank you for agreeing to help us."

"Of course. Anything for an old friend." She smiled, her gaze lingering on him before turning to Damien. "Let's get him inside, shall we?"

They carried Damien into the cozy living room, where Erin retrieved a small vial from the shelf.

"This will put him to sleep for a while," she explained as she expertly cast a potent sleeping spell over Damien.

His breathing instantly deepened, his massive form completely relaxed.

"Good," Erin said, satisfied. "Now, let's talk about taming his wolf."

Nina joined them, listening intently as Erin described the process in detail.

"First, we'll need to establish a bond between Damien and his wolf," Erin began. "That means helping him understand his wolf's instincts, fears, and desires. Once he can communicate with his wolf on a deeper level, they'll be able to work together harmoniously."

"Sounds intense," Nina commented, her brow furrowed in concern.

"It is," Erin confirmed. "But it's necessary for Damien's wellbeing. And I'm confident we can help him."

As Erin spoke, she moved with fluid grace, her presence commanding the room. Even though she was discussing a complex and dangerous task, her confidence was unwavering.

It was the prowess and determination Killian had always remembered about Erin. It reminded him of their past together – a time when passion and love had intertwined them like vines.

"Excuse us for a moment," Killian said, drawing Erin aside into another room.

He needed answers, and he needed them now.

"Erin," he began, trying to control the emotions

surging through him. "I have to ask... why did you agree to help me? After all this time?"

"Because I never forgot the time we spent together," she confessed, her eyes searching his. "And because I know you're still the same caring, strong man I once knew."

"Erin," Killian whispered, feeling the weight of his past with her bearing down on him. "You must understand that I can't take our relationship to the next level. I think you deserve better than what I can offer."

"Killian..." Erin's voice trailed off as she reached out to touch his arm, her fingers brushing against the rough fabric of his shirt.

The contact sent shivers racing up his spine, awakening a desire that had long lain dormant.

"Besides," Killian continued, forcing himself to focus. "I'm happy that you've settled here and found a home."

"Is that truly what you want?" Erin asked, her eyes glistening with unshed tears. "For us to simply forget our past and move on?"

"Maybe it's for the best," Killian replied, his heart aching with the painful truth of his words. He knew that even if their paths had crossed again, the spark between them could never be reignited. The fire that once burned so brightly had been reduced to embers, and it was time to let go.

Erin's breath trembled as she leaned in to kiss Killian, the sultry scent of her perfume filling his senses.

She was undeniably captivating.

But there was something else as well. An energy, palpable in the atmosphere.

But before their lips could meet, Killian caught sight of a dark bruise on her neck, partially hidden by her coppery curls. He stepped back abruptly, his heart pounding in his chest.

"Erin, what happened?" he demanded, his voice barely more than a growl.

The stench of injuries emanating from her skin sent his wolf snarling inside him. His anger ignited like wildfire, and with careful hands, he peeled her shirt off, revealing a canvas of bruises marring her porcelain skin.

"Who did this to you?" Killian's eyes burned with a fierce rage that threatened to consume him.

A storm brewed within him, fueled by his failure to protect Erin—the woman who had once been his everything.

"Vincent," he snarled, fighting the urge to go after her husband right then and there. "Tell me it was him."

Erin hesitated for a moment, tears threatening to spill over her emerald eyes.

"Look, Killian, there's nothing you can do about it," she said, her voice strained as she tried to maintain her composure. "Let's forget about all this, okay?"

The sound of footsteps approaching alerted them both to Nina's presence. She entered the room, her eyes widening at the sight of Erin's half-naked body and the tension that hung heavy between them.

"Hey, what's going on here?" Nina asked cautiously, taking in the scene before her.

"Nothing much," Erin replied with forced nonchalance, attempting to conceal her vulnerability with a casual smirk. "I'm just Killian's fuck buddy. This is how we usually hang out."

"Erin!" Killian barked, his anger reaching new heights. "Don't make light of this situation. You're hurt, and I won't stand for it."

"Killian, stop," Erin pleaded, her eyes pleading with him to let the matter go. "I don't need your help. I can handle this on my own. Please leave."

"Like hell you will handle this on your own!" Killian roared, his fists clenched by his sides.

The emotional turmoil he felt threatened to rip him apart. He couldn't bear the thought of leaving Erin to suffer at the hands of her abusive husband, but forcing her to leave against her will was not an option either.

"Please, just go," Erin whispered, tears finally sliding down her cheeks. "I can't bear to see you like this."

"Erin, I can't just walk away," Killian said, his voice ragged with pain. "You were once mine, and I still care for you more than you know."

"Then show me you care," she implored, desperation lacing her words. "Show me you care by letting me make my own choices, even if they're wrong."

"Even if it kills you?" Killian countered, the weight of his love for her and his duty as a protector crushing his resolve.

"Especially if it kills me," Erin replied, her voice barely audible.

"Fine," Killian ground out, his voice like sandpaper. "But we're not leaving you here alone." He turned to Nina, who had been watching the exchange with wide eyes. "Pack up the pets. I'll handle Damien."

Nina nodded, her jaw set in determination. Killian bent down and hoisted the unconscious wolf form of Damien onto his broad shoulders, wincing slightly at the weight. As he carried Damien out to the car, he glanced back at Erin.

"Come with us, Erin," he pleaded one last time. "Let me protect you."

"Go to hell, Killian!" Erin spat, her fiery eyes flashing with anger, belying the hurt beneath. "Leave me alone."

Killian's heart clenched at her words, but he refused to let her see how much they affected him. With a heavy sigh, he placed Damien in the back seat of the car, arranging him as comfortably as possible.

He turned to Nina, who was finishing up with the other animals.

"Stay guard," he instructed, his voice firm despite the turmoil inside him. "I'm going back for Erin."

"Be careful," Nina warned, her gaze sympathetic.

When Killian reentered the house, he found Erin standing defiantly in the living room, her arms crossed over her chest.

"Erin, please," Killian begged, his voice cracking. "Don't do this to yourself. To us."

"Us?" she scoffed bitterly. "There is no 'us,' Killian. There never will be again."

"Then think of yourself," he countered, his frustration mounting. "You deserve better than this. You deserve better than him."

"Stop trying to save me!" she yelled, her own frustration boiling over. "I don't need you!"

"Damn it, Erin!" Killian roared, his pain a living,

breathing thing threatening to suffocate him. "I can't lose you again!"

As if on cue, Nina burst into the room, a tranq gun in her hand. Without hesitation, she aimed it at Erin and pulled the trigger.

The dart struck Erin's shoulder, and her eyes widened in shock as the drug took effect. She swayed for a moment before collapsing into unconsciousness.

"I'm so sorry," Nina muttered, her voice quivering as she gazed down at Erin's still silhouette. "I don't do martial arts like Ivy. But I've been dealing with a lot of pets and one very temperamental werewolf, so I carry this gun around with me. This is the first time it has ever been fired."

"Thank you, Nina," Killian said quietly.

He scooped Erin's limp body into his arms, cradling her tenderly against his chest.

"Let's go," he told Nina, his voice barely audible. "We've done all we can for now."

THE HEADLIGHTS of Killian's car pierced through the inky darkness as they sped down the winding road. The tension in the vehicle was palpable, an unspoken current of emotions that threatened to drown them all. Nina glanced at him from the passenger seat, her expression a mixture of concern and curiosity.

"Killian," she began hesitantly, "are your feelings for Ivy real?"

He gripped the steering wheel tighter, his knuckles

turning white. The question caught him off-guard, but he knew there was no point in evading it.

"Yes," he admitted, his voice strained. "They're too real to be good."

Nina watched him closely, her gaze probing. "What do you mean?"

"We're too different," he said, his gaze fixed on the road ahead. "I have responsibilities with my people, and as an alpha, I can't afford to be selfish. I don't know how to make it work."

"Maybe you don't have to figure it out alone," Nina suggested gently, her eyes filled with empathy. "You and Ivy could find a solution together."

Killian shook his head, feeling the weight of his curse heavy on his shoulders. "I need to break free from this curse before I can even think about a future with her."

Silence settled between them, punctuated only by the steady hum of the car's engine and the soft whirring of tires on asphalt. Nina seemed to mull over his words, her brow furrowed in thought. Finally, she broke the silence again.

"What about Erin?" she asked, her voice soft. "How do you feel about her?"

"Erin is...a good friend," Killian replied, struggling to keep his voice steady.

Images of Erin's bruised body flashed through his mind, igniting a storm of anger and guilt inside him. He didn't tell Nina that deep down, he was unsure whether he could protect either of his women, Ivy or Erin. The thought gnawed at him, a constant reminder of his own limitations.

"Sometimes, it's hard to see the line between friendship and something more," Nina observed, her eyes searching his face for an answer. "Especially when you've shared so much with someone."

"True," Killian mumbled, his grip on the steering wheel relaxing slightly.

His heart ached for both Ivy and Erin, the two women who had captured his soul in different ways. But he knew that love alone wouldn't be enough to save them from the danger that loomed over their lives – a danger that he, as an alpha, was duty-bound to face head-on.

As they continued their journey towards the sanctuary, Killian vowed to do everything in his power to protect those he cared for most. But in the darkest recesses of his mind, doubt lingered, threatening to consume him from within.

A SUDDEN FLASH of headlights in the rearview mirror caught Killian's attention, and his heart clenched with a mixture of dread and fury. Vincent's sleek black car roared into view, followed by two more vehicles filled with his menacing pack.

"Damn it," Killian muttered under his breath as he floored the accelerator, gripping the wheel tighter. He could feel the tension radiating from Nina beside him, her fingers curling around the tranq gun in her lap.

"Looks like we've got company," Nina said through

gritted teeth, her eyes fixed on the approaching cars in the side mirror.

"Stay here and protect Erin," Killian instructed as he swung the car onto the shoulder of the road, tires screeching on the asphalt. He stepped out, his body coiled with pent-up rage and the weight of responsibility bearing down on him.

"Killian!" Vincent sneered, his voice dripping with malice as he emerged from his car. "You think you can just kill my brother and walk away?"

"Your brother was a threat to everyone around him," Killian growled, meeting Vincent's gaze head-on. "I did what I had to do to keep my people safe."

"Safe?" Vincent laughed mockingly. "You're pathetic, hiding behind your pack like a coward."

"Call me what you will, but I'm not the one taking out my anger on an innocent woman," Killian shot back, thinking of Erin's bruised and battered body.

"Ah, yes, dear Erin," Vincent drawled, smirking as if he knew exactly how deep Killian's feelings for her ran. "I knew you couldn't resist getting involved, being the hero. But guess what? You can't save everyone, especially when you're so weak yourself."

The taunt stung, and Killian's blood boiled hotter. He knew that Vincent was right – he couldn't shift into his wolf form due to the curse, and that put him at a disadvantage. But he refused to let fear or self-doubt control him.

"Killian might be weakened," Nina's voice rang out as she stepped out of the car, her tranq gun raised and aimed at Vincent, "but he's not alone."

"Pathetic," Vincent spat, grabbing one of his men and shoving him in front of the dart that flew from Nina's weapon.

"Say what you want about me, but don't underestimate my pack," Killian warned, his voice low and dangerous. "We are strong, and we stand together. Can you say the same for your group of misfits?"

Vincent's eyes darkened with fury, but he hesitated, knowing that Killian spoke the truth. His pack was weak and disorganized, no match for the united force of the Kyneton pack.

"Mark my words, Killian," Vincent threatened, slowly backing away. "If you or any of your precious pack set foot outside your territory, I'll make sure you're hunted down like the animals you are."

"Go ahead and try," Killian replied icily, his gaze never wavering from Vincent's retreating figure.

As the enemy cars sped away, Killian took a deep breath, trying to silence the doubts that gnawed at his resolve.

He knew that the battle was far from over.

# EIGHT

Ivy's heart raced as she frantically dialed Killian's number for the third time, each attempt met with the same infuriating silence.

Her breaths came in short, anxious bursts as she glanced around the desolate landscape, feeling the weight of Patrick's connection to Killian's late father pressing down on her like a heavy fog.

She knew it was somehow tied to the curse on Killian, but she couldn't reach him. The urgency gnawed at her insides, threatening to consume her.

"Damn it," she muttered under her breath, her fingers trembling as she clutched her phone.

Desperation drove her to scale a nearby boulder, hoping for even the faintest signal from such a height. But as she reached the top, her phone remained as lifeless as the barren land surrounding her.

"Come on, come on," she hissed through gritted teeth, trying various spots on the boulder, but still finding no cell connection. The deep-seated dread in her chest grew more unbearable by the second.

In the end, she tried Ciaran's cell phone.

It worked like magic. Relief washed over her like a warm wave, but it did little to quell the storm of emotions inside her.

"Finally," Ivy breathed out, her voice shaking with relief and frustration. "Ciaran, I can't get to Killian. So, I tried your number."

"Ah, Ivy," Ciaran's smooth voice greeted her. "You finally figured out that Killian's technology is primitive. The number I gave you uses my private network connection – it's one of a kind."

"Listen," Ivy urged, her heart pounding against her ribs. "I found a picture in Patrick's cave with three men. Patrick, Ayden and Desmond. Patrick knew Ayden. That means Fiona might know Quinn. But they never talked about it. I think this relationship between the men has something to do with Killian's pack and the curse."

"Interesting," Ciaran mused, his tone shifting to one of curiosity. "Patrick, Ayden, and Desmond, you say? They may be part of a triad secret that the LeBlancs never spoke of."

"Triad secret. That's it." Ivy's grip tightened on the phone, her interest piqued. "What do you know?"

"Supernatural triads are formed when three individuals with unique abilities swear loyalty to each other. It's said to create a powerful bond and amplify their powers," Ciaran explained, his voice low and cautious.

"Could that have something to do with Killian's

curse?" Ivy questioned, her mind racing with the implications.

"Perhaps," Ciaran replied cryptically. "We'll need more information to be sure."

"Right," Ivy agreed, determination surging through her veins. "I'll keep digging. I just hope we figure this out in time."

"Before you go, Ivy," Ciaran interjected, his voice taking on a more serious tone. "I need you to search for any artifacts in Patrick's cave that may lead to dark magic and the magical realm. It could help us understand the triad secret better."

Ivy hesitated, unsure if she wanted to delve deeper into the cave's secrets, but knowing it was crucial to breaking Killian's curse. "All right, I'll see what I can find," she agreed.

"Good luck, Ivy," Ciaran said, before hanging up.

Ivy slipped her phone into her pocket and turned her attention to the breathtaking view at the top of the boulder.

As her gaze traveled down, she spotted Fiona waiting for her at the foot of the massive rock. In that moment, something caught her eye – a patch of white daisies, each with one blue petal, nestled between the rocks below.

A jolt of recognition coursed through her; these were the same flowers that had haunted Killian's mother when she was cursed for years.

Ivy furrowed her brows, wondering how she'd never noticed them during her training in these very mountains.

"Are those...?" Fiona trailed off as she too noticed the peculiar blossoms.

"White daisies with one blue petal," Ivy murmured, a shiver running down her spine as she carefully descended the boulder. "I've heard about them. They're connected to Killian's mother."

As she reached the ground, Ivy noticed the dramatic change in Fiona's expression.

Her eyes widened, and her lips parted slightly, as if something magical had taken hold of her senses.

Fiona tilted her head back, releasing an unearthly sound that made Ivy's hair stand on end.

The eerie melody reverberated through the air, sending tremors down Ivy's spine.

She stared at Fiona, her heart pounding in her chest as she tried to decipher the meaning behind the strange sound. It felt as though it bore the weight of ancient magic, a whisper from another realm that resonated deep within Ivy's soul.

"Fi...Fiona? Mom .." Ivy stammered, taking a cautious step toward the older woman. "What was that?"

Fiona blinked, as if awakening from a trance, and shook her head. "I... I don't know," she admitted, her voice barely above a whisper. "But something about these flowers stirred something within me, something I can't quite explain."

Ivy glanced back at the daisies, unease creeping up her spine. She knew they were somehow linked to the curse on Killian's family, and she couldn't shake the feeling that they held secrets she was yet to uncover.

"Let's get back to that cave," Ivy said, determination lacing her words. "We have a lot of work ahead of us."

***

No sooner had Fiona's unearthly sound faded than the quiet of the mountains was disturbed by a rustling in the underbrush. A pack of red foxes emerged from the shadows, their eyes gleaming with an unnatural malevolence.

Ivy's pulse quickened as she stared down at the creatures, noting the unnatural way they moved - it was as if something sinister had taken hold of them.

"Stay up there!" Fiona shouted, her voice surprisingly commanding.

There was a new authority in her tone that Ivy had never heard before, and despite feeling a burning need to help, she found herself obeying without question.

"Climb up onto the boulder!" Fiona yelled.

"I... No..." Ivy tried to resist, but Fiona used her otherworldly strength to lift her body halfway onto the boulder. She clung on tightly, feeling both terrified and in awe of Fiona's power. It was something she had never seen before; it was both strong and frightening.

Ivy watched, her breath caught in her throat, as Fiona closed her eyes and took a deep breath.

She could see her body trembling, as if battling an internal force. Then, with a suddenness that made Ivy gasp, Fiona's form began to shift and ripple. Her bones cracked and reformed, her skin sprouted thick fur, and her face elongated into a sleek muzzle.

Before Ivy's astonished eyes, Fiona transformed into a magnificent lynx.

The foxes hesitated for a moment, their eyes flickering between Fiona and Ivy, who clung to the boulder above. It was clear they hadn't anticipated facing such a formidable opponent. Yet, driven by whatever dark force controlled them, they continued to surge forward.

"Protect yourself, Ivy!" Fiona called out, her voice now a guttural growl that sent shivers down Ivy's spine. "I'll deal with them!"

As Fiona leaped into action, her powerful muscles propelling her toward the encroaching foxes, Ivy tried to steady her racing heart. She focused on pulling energy from the earth beneath her, forming a protective shield around herself while keeping a watchful eye on the battle below.

She marveled at Fiona's prowess as the older woman – now a fierce, agile lynx – tore through the pack with ruthless efficiency.

It was a side of Fiona Ivy had never seen before, and it both awed and terrified her.

The foxes were no match for Fiona's ferocity, and they quickly fell to her swift and lethal blows. But there were so many foxes.

The snarls and growls of the foxes filled the air, as they circled Fiona, their red eyes gleaming with malevolence.

Ivy started to climb down.

"Stay up there. Don't distract me."

Ivy gripped the edge of the boulder, her knuckles white, as she watched Fiona dart and weave between the snapping jaws, her powerful lynx form a blur of deadly grace.

Fiona roared, her voice echoing through the mountains. The warning only seemed to enrage the foxes further, and they lunged at her in unison, determined to bring her down.

But Fiona was a force of nature, unleashed after years of suppression.

Her claws tore through fur and flesh, while her fangs found throats and snapped spines with brutal efficiency. In mere moments, the pack was decimated – each lifeless body splayed across the rocky terrain, a testament to Fiona's prowess.

Panting heavily, Fiona surveyed the carnage around her before turning her gaze back up to Ivy. She shifted back into her human form, naked and vulnerable, her dark hair matted with sweat and blood.

"Are you okay? Can I come down now?" Ivy called out, her voice wavering.

Fiona nodded, her eyes weary but resolute. "Yes, we need to talk."

With a final glance at the slain foxes, Ivy climbed down from the boulder and approached Fiona.

"Here," Ivy said, offering her jacket to Fiona. As Fiona wrapped it around herself, she sighed, visibly steeling herself for the conversation that was about to unfold.

"Why did you keep this hidden? That you can shift into...that?"

"Because I didn't want this life, Ivy," Fiona admitted,

anguish clouding her features. "I didn't want the power or the responsibility that came with being part of Quinn's pack. I just wanted a quiet life – a normal one."

"Patrick promised me that," she continued, her voice thick with emotion. "He said he'd protect me with his magic, and I wouldn't have to be involved in the supernatural world anymore. So, I buried my abilities deep within me, hoping they'd never resurface."

Ivy's heart ached for Fiona, understanding the burden that had been placed upon her shoulders. "But why didn't you tell me? We could have faced this together."

"Because I was afraid," Fiona whispered, tears glistening in her eyes. "Afraid of what it might mean for you if you knew the truth. Afraid of who I truly am."

"But now you know," she finished, her gaze meeting Ivy's. "And we need to find out what's going on – why these cursed flowers are growing again, and what it means for Killian and his family."

"Let's do this together. We'll figure this out, and put an end to whatever evil is at play here."

Fiona offered a small, grateful smile.

Ivy's nerves were still rattled as she watched Fiona, the woman who had raised her, trying to regain her composure after the gruesome scene that had just unfolded.

Ivy couldn't help but wonder what other secrets lay buried within their family. She needed answers, and there was no better time to ask than now.

"Tell me about the triad," Ivy began hesitantly, her voice barely audible over the rustling of the wind in the trees. "You mentioned Patrick, Ayden, and Desmond — what's their connection?"

Fiona sighed deeply, rubbing her temples as if trying to ward off a headache. "They were good friends once, like brothers in arms. But when Ayden was killed, it tore them apart. Desmond vanished without a trace, and Patrick... well, you know his story. He withdrew to the cave. And Quinn lost her sanity."

"Did Patrick blame himself for not being able to save Ayden?"

"I don't know, Ivy." Her eyes clouded with sadness. "He was devastated by the loss. I tried to comfort him, but he kept pushing everyone away, including me."

"Is that why he never had children of his own?" Ivy questioned, her heart heavy with the revelation.

"Actually," Fiona took a deep breath, preparing herself for the truth, "he thought he couldn't have children. That's one of the reasons he withdrew." She looked at Ivy, her eyes filled with sorrow. "So, I adopted you. I chose Katrina Murdoch ..."

Fiona's voice trailed off, her eyes rolled back and then she crumpled to the ground.

DEAR READER, PLEASE DOWNLOAD THE COMPLETE -EBOOK HERE

Fiona's body convulsed as she shifted back into her lynx form, her cries morphing into inhuman sounds of fear and confusion. The fur on her back stood on end, and her dilated eyes darted around their surroundings. She seemed to be losing her mind, the drift happening fast and uncontrolled.

"Easy, Mom," Ivy said, trying to stay calm despite the tense situation. "I've got you."

Using her basic survival instinct, Fiona clung to Ivy for protection, her claws digging into Ivy's jacket. The snarls and hisses that escaped her throat were primal and menacing, a warning to any creatures or animals lurking nearby.

"Stay with me, Mom," Ivy urged, her heart pounding as she held onto the now feral lynx. "You can fight this."

As they stood there, Ivy noticed a change in Fiona's demeanor and behavior.

Her eyes flickered with the fading remnants of human intelligence, as if her mind was being taken away from her and she was resisting it with every ounce of strength she had left.

This was the work of dark magic.

"Damn it," Ivy whispered, recognizing the magical signature.

It was the same kind that had reaped the tiger out of Killian's mother, Quinn, preventing her from shifting and being in control of her mind for years. Fiona was fighting to hang on to her animal.

That is why she had shifted into a lynx again.

"Listen to me, Mom," Ivy said urgently, gripping the lynx's face in her hands. "You have to remember who you are. You're stronger than this darkness."

Fiona blinked at her, the recognition in her gaze fleeting but present. Ivy knew that their time was running out, and she needed to act quickly before Fiona was lost to the darkness forever.

"Come on, we need to get you away from here," Ivy said, pulling Fiona along with her as she scanned the area for a safe place to take refuge.

Ivy's PULSE raced as she noticed the white daisies with single blue petals scattered around them. Her instincts screamed that these flowers were the source of the dark magic affecting Fiona, draining her energy and threatening to consume her mind.

"Stay away from those flowers," Ivy warned, glancing at the lynx. Fiona's ears twitched, acknowledging Ivy's words despite her inability to speak.

"Come on, we need to move!" Ivy urged, her voice laced with determination.

She led the way, guiding Fiona towards the car parked further down the mountain path.

As they ran, they faced numerous obstacles - jagged rocks jutting out from the ground, thorny bushes clawing at their clothes and fur, and the uneven terrain making it difficult to maintain their footing.

Ivy's heart pounded in her chest as she dodged and weaved through the treacherous landscape, all while trying to keep Fiona close.

"Almost there, Mom! Hang on!" Ivy called out, catching glimpses of the car between the trees.

Fiona's breaths came in ragged gasps as she struggled to keep up, her feline form not as adept at traversing the rocky terrain as Ivy. But she pressed on, understanding the urgency in Ivy's tone.

Finally, they reached the car, which seemed like a beacon of hope amidst the chaos surrounding them. Ivy quickly unlocked the door and motioned for Fiona to jump inside.

"Get in, now!" she commanded, her gaze darting back to the ominous flowers creeping closer.

Fiona obeyed, leaping into the backseat of the car with surprising grace.

"Okay, we're safe for now," Ivy muttered, sliding behind the steering wheel. Her hands gripped the wheel tightly, knuckles turning white as she started the engine. "But we need to find a way to break this dark magic's hold on you."

THE MOMENT Ivy and Fiona left the car park, it became apparent that the sinister flowers had begun to spread their influence beyond their initial location.

They were everywhere.

They seemed to grow from the ground as she drove the car on winding dirt roads exiting the forrest.

As if on cue, the forest erupted into chaos. Birds screeched overhead, their once harmonious songs replaced by discordant cries. Squirrels darted through the trees, their eyes glazed with panic. Even larger creatures like deer and foxes stumbled out of the underbrush, disoriented and aggressive.

"Stay with me, don't look at the flowers, don't even think about them, Mom.

Ivy instructed as she drove out of the National park, approaching the territory of civilization.

Ivy's heart raced as they reached the highway, her eyes scanning for any sign of danger.

A wave of dread washed over her when she noticed the daisies beginning to sprout along the roadside. The sinister flowers seemed to taunt her, their blue petals standing out starkly against the white.

"Mom, do you see that?" Ivy asked, her voice shaky with concern.

Fiona's golden eyes locked onto the daisies, and she let out a low growl, her body tense and ready for action, and she shifted back into human form. "I see them," she replied through clenched teeth. "This isn't good."

The sound of screeching tires tore through the air, snapping Ivy's attention back to the road.

Ivy watched in horror as cars swerved erratically, narrowly missing one another as drivers struggled to maintain control.

"We need to get away from these flowers before more people get hurt." Ivy muttered, her knuckles turning white as she gripped the steering wheel.

"Watch out!" Fiona yelled as a car careened towards them. Ivy slammed on the brakes, her heart leaping into her throat as the vehicle skidded past, inches from colliding with their own.

"Are you okay?" Ivy asked, her voice trembling.

"Fine," Fiona gasped, her breaths coming in quick pants. "Just keep driving."

As they continued down the highway, the scene around them grew increasingly chaotic. Cars fishtailed and spun out of control, their drivers clearly affected by the dark magic emanating from the daisies. Ivy's mind raced as she tried to come up with a plan to protect both her mother and the innocent bystanders caught in the crossfire.

"Can you help them?" Fiona asked, her voice barely audible over the cacophony of honking horns and screeching tires.

"Let me try something," Ivy said, her brow furrowed in concentration. She began to mutter an incantation under her breath. She cast healing magic toward the general direction of the city.

"Did it work?" Fiona asked, her eyes wide with hope.

"Only temporarily," Ivy admitted, her chest tight-

ening with frustration. "We need to find a more perma-
nent solution. We need to go to the Sanctuary."

With the chaos of the highway receding behind them,
Ivy glanced in the rearview mirror.

"Lyrisa," Ivy whispered, her voice cracking under the
weight of fear and desperation. "I need your help."

In response to her plea, a faint shimmering appeared
in the air above them, growing more solid until it
coalesced into the ethereal form of the minor deity
Lyrisa.

"Please," Ivy continued, her hands gripping the
steering wheel so tightly her knuckles turned white.
"You see what's going on. Just tell me how to fix it
..."

"Dark magic is at work here," Lyrisa said solemnly,
her voice echoing through the car like a haunting
melody. "There is only one place that can offer you
protection right now: the Sanctuary."

"That's where we're heading."

"Then you are on the right path. What do you need
my guidance for?"

"What is driving the world insane? Not dark magic,
I'm aware of that. Is there anything specific I can do to
try and fix it?"

"Your engagement with the Underworld caused this
..."

"Hey I didn't want to engage. Selene dragged me
there."

"You requested the explanation. I'm elucidating it to you. I am not indicting you of anything."

"What would be the solution then?"

"Apart from adhering to or resolving your dealings with Selene and the Underworld, I do not know of any other solution."

"All right. It seems I have no choice but seeing this through. And I'll do it my way."

Lyrisa nodded solemnly before disappearing in a shimmer of moonlight, leaving Ivy and Fiona alone once more on their treacherous journey toward the Sanctuary.

As Ivy sped down the darkened highway, she gripped the steering wheel with white-knuckled intensity. The wind howled around them, and the eerie glow of the moon cast ominous shadows across the road.

"Can't this thing go any faster?" Fiona asked, her voice tense as she peered through the windshield, searching for any signs of danger ahead.

"Trust me, I'm pushing it to the limit," Ivy replied, gritting her teeth as she navigated through obstacles and avoided debris that littered the road.

As she veered onto the trail that snaked through the woods surrounding the Sanctuary, a man suddenly materialized in her path. She screeched to an abrupt halt, just feet away from crashing into him.

Ivy parked and stepped out of the car. "If you want to die, go to the highway right now," she dared them. "Don't put a dent in my car!"

A tall man stood in the center of the clearing. She could tell he was a werewolf, before he even shifted. "Well, well, who would have thought—this is the woman working with Killian to kill my brother. Odds are not in your favor. He banned my people from coming onto these territories. But guess what? You'll need to make another fifteen feet to get to that border. Here it's public ground and I'm hunting with my men. Nobody can blame me for mistaking you for a deer."

"You're Vincent?"

"Yes, indeed I am. My brother's death wasn't your fault. But too bad you're with Killian. I'll do whatever it takes to make him feel the pain. I married his ex-girl-friend and tortured her every day so that she feeds the information back to him. That's why he ventured into my territory to take her away. Now, it is official: he stole my woman from my home. I'm going to take his."

"I'm nobody's woman. I need to go that way," she stated firmly, pointing a determined finger at the dark road ahead of her. "If you're in my way, you'll have to negotiate with my car."

Without warning, Vincent charged towards her with a menacing sneer on his face. Ivy was not one to back down from a fight, and this was the perfect opportunity to unleash all her pent-up anger. She spun around grace-fully and kicked him square in the jaw with a roundhouse kick that would make even the most seasoned martial artist proud. The impact resonated throughout the night air, and she could feel her foot throbbing with pain as he stumbled backwards, clutching his bleeding mouth.

He grinned wickedly, admiring her ferocity despite his injury. "I like a fierce woman," he said through swollen lips.

"I don't like scumbags."

He was about to charge at her again when a small shadow of a pup darted out from the woods and bit his leg.

"Ouch, what the fuck!"

"Oh no." Ivy groaned. She recognized the dark brown mutt whose mother she accidentally killed. The pup wanted revenge on her and wouldn't like the idea that Vincent got to her first.

As vicious as it was, the little puppy had no idea it had bitten a dangerous werewolf. Vincent grabbed the pup by its neck fur. He would break its neck with one shake and the pup would join its mother in death.

She pulled out the small knife she kept on her ankle just in case and with one throw, it pierced at his jugular. He let go of the little dog who slipped away before getting caught in the crossfire between his new enemy and his old one.

Vincent roared as he started to shift.

Ivy had no hope of standing up to Vincent in his werewolf form.

She had only one chance and she had to act fast.

Closing her eyes, she concentrated with all her might, reaching out her hands and yanking at the wolf spirit that inhabited his body, in the same way she did with Killian before.

But this time it was different. Instead of separating

him from his wolf spirit, Ivy pulled out Vincent's soul instead.

His wolf spirit howled in confusion as it bounded away and Vincent's soul hovered above his body in a state of shock.

Ivy looked back down at her hands, realizing the gravity of what she'd done: she had just reaped a man's soul in one swift move and killed both him and his wolf spirit.

Fear filled her being - what kind of monster had she become?

# TEN

Killian stepped into the dimly lit Sanctuary, his heart pounding in his chest.

He read the text message with dread: Ivy was all alone in Patrick's cave, exposed to the vile beast he had encountered on the mountain. His heart raced as he saw that she had attempted to reach him, but for some reason her signal hadn't been sent through.

Then her final text said she was alright.

Once again, he had been unable to provide for her safety, and she managed to persevere despite any difficulties that she might have faced. She never really relied on his protection. On the other hand, he could very well need hers.

"Killian, I have an idea," Ciaran approached."We can use the LeBlancs' facilities in Melbourne to gather information about the creature you saw..."

As Ciaran spoke, Killian noticed the subtle shift in his cousin's tone and body language when Erin entered the room. There was a tightness in his voice, a guarded quality that hadn't been there before.

Ciaran didn't trust Erin.

"Sounds like a plan," Killian replied, treading carefully between Ciaran and Erin. "But we need to act fast."

"Of course," Ciaran agreed, his eyes darting towards Erin for a split second before returning to Killian. "Time is of the essence."

"Is everything all right?" Erin asked, a hint of concern in her voice as she picked up on the tension between the two men.

"Everything's fine," Killian reassured her, though his thoughts were racing. He knew he had to trust Ciaran's instincts, but he couldn't shake the feeling that Erin was genuinely invested in helping them. And despite their complicated history, he still cared for her deeply.

"Let's get started then," Ciaran said, forcing a smile as he turned towards the door. "The sooner we find answers, the better."

As they moved through the Sanctuary, Killian stole glances at Erin, trying to gauge her thoughts.

She seemed focused, determined, and entirely present in the moment. He wanted to believe in her, but he knew better than to dismiss Ciaran's concerns outright.

"I hope you weren't too upset that we tranq you to get you here."

Erin smiled. "Not at all. I wasn't thinking straight. I know you're worried about Ivy, but I promise you, I'll do my best to help."

"Thank you," Killian replied quietly, offering her a

small smile before turning his attention back to their mission.

Killian stood in the dimly lit hallway, his heart still heavy with the weight of Ivy's absence and Ciaran's distrust of Erin. But he couldn't dwell on those thoughts now; there were more pressing matters at hand.

"Listen, Ciaran," Killian said, pulling his cousin aside. "I need you to stay here one more night. Vincent — Adam's little brother — threatened us on our way here. It's too dangerous for you and Viv to leave tonight."

Ciaran hesitated for a moment before nodding, his jaw set with determination. "All right, we'll stay. We can't risk any more trouble."

"Thank you." Killian clapped Ciaran on the shoulder, grateful for his understanding.

As they made their way back to the main area, Nina approached them, her eyes filled with curiosity. "Viv," she said, addressing the young druid, "have you ever met a mage's familiar before?"

Viv shook her head, her expression wary but intrigued.

"Come on, then," Nina beckoned, leading her toward a cozy corner where three animals lounged on plush cushions.

Killian watched as Viv knelt down beside the Cavoodle, Snuggleworth, who wagged his tail enthusiastically. The husky, Pixy, and gummy cat, Simba, also perked up at her presence.

"Snuggleworth is a natural-born healer, Ivy met him at he Dubai airport," Nina explained, stroking the dog's fur. "Pixy specializes in protection spells, Ivy rescued her on a mission in the highland woods, and Simba... well, he's still figuring it out."

Viv's eyes widened with awe as she reached out to pet the creatures. Killian felt a warmth spread through him as he witnessed Vivian's walls slowly crumbling. For a moment, she seemed like an innocent teenager, captivated by the magical world around her.

"Thank you for showing me," Viv whispered, her voice soft and full of wonder.

"Of course," Nina replied, a bright smile lighting up her face. "You're part of our family now."

As Killian observed the scene unfolding before him, a sense of relief washed over him despite the dangers they faced and the many secrets that still needed to be uncovered.

There was a sense of unity and camaraderie in the room. For the first time in a long while, he allowed himself to believe that maybe – just maybe – everything would work out in the end.

***

THE FOLLOWING MORNING, Killian stood at the edge of the training grounds, watching intently as Erin worked her magic on Damien's wolf.

He was anxious because Ivy hadn't arrived at the Sanctuary yet. But he didn't want to distract her with a call.

The massive creature paced back and forth in front of

Erin, its silver fur bristling with tension, hackles raised, and teeth bared in a snarl. Erin remained calm and collected, holding her ground and locking eyes with the beast, asserting her dominance.

"Easy, boy," she crooned, her voice firm but gentle. "We're not here to hurt you."

Killian's heart raced as he observed the scene, his fingers flexing at his sides.

It was crucial that he be present during the process, since Damien had been turned by his blood. He could feel the connection between them, an almost tangible thread that bound their fates together.

As much as he wanted to maintain his distance and let Erin work, he couldn't help but worry about the outcome.

"Erin seems to know what she's doing," Ciaran murmured from beside him, mirroring Killian's thoughts.

"Damien means a lot to me," Killian admitted, his voice barely above a whisper. "I can't afford for this to go wrong."

"Trust her, Killian. You said she's one of the best," Ciaran reassured him, placing a hand on his shoulder.

Killian nodded, forcing himself to take a deep breath. He knew that Erin was skilled in taming wolves. He'd seen her do it countless times before, but this was different. This time, it was personal.

He watched as Erin slowly approached the snarling wolf, her steps deliberate and measured. She reached out one hand, palm facing the beast, and continued her low, soothing words. "I'm here to help you, Damien. We all are."

The wolf hesitated, its amber eyes flicking from Erin's outstretched hand to her face, and then back again. Killian held his breath, praying for a breakthrough.

"Come on, Damien," Erin encouraged gently, never breaking eye contact. "You can do this."

In that moment, the wolf seemed to make a decision. It took a tentative step forward, its snarl subsiding ever so slightly. Erin remained still, allowing the wolf to come to her.

As the wolf finally placed its muzzle in Erin's palm, a wave of relief washed over Killian. He knew they had reached a critical point in the taming process, and it was all thanks to Erin's skill and patience.

"Good boy," Erin praised, stroking the wolf's fur as it leaned into her touch.

"That's incredible," Ciaran commented, echoing Killian's thoughts once more.

Killian nodded, and said nothing.

Now that the initial hurdle had been overcome, Killian knew the rest of the taming process would be smoother.

***

. . .

THE SUN HAD DIPPED below the horizon, painting the sky in hues of deep purple and gold as Killian made his way to his mother's quarters.

The Sanctuary was quiet, the air heavy with the unsaid words that hung between him and Erin. But this moment wasn't about them; it was about seeking answers to questions that had haunted him for years.

"Mother?" he called softly, rapping on the door before entering.

Quinn reclined on an ornate chaise lounge, her once vibrant red hair now faded to a dull russet, streaked with silver. Her eyes, still sharp and intelligent, held a weariness that hadn't been there in her youth.

She glanced at her son and smiled, her face lighting up despite the lines etched into her skin.

"Killian, my boy," she said warmly. "What brings you to me?"

"Mother, I need to ask you something." Killian hesitated, fearing that his questions might be too much for her frail state. "About Father..."

"What do you want to know?" Quinn sighed, her gaze drifting to a portrait hanging on the wall – a younger, stronger version of herself standing next to a tall, powerful man with piercing blue eyes.

"Mother, do you remember anything... unusual about that night?" Killian asked cautiously, not wanting to cause her distress.

"Unusual?" She frowned, her brow furrowing as she tried to recall the memories buried beneath years of pain and sorrow. "I... I can't remember much, my dear. It's all a blur... I'm sorry."

"Please, don't apologize," Killian reassured her, his heart aching as he watched her struggle with the past. "You've been through so much."

"Have faith, Killian," Quinn whispered, reaching out a trembling hand to cup her son's cheek. "The truth will reveal itself when the time is right."

"Thank you, Mother," he said, pressing a gentle kiss to her knuckles before taking his leave.

***

Determined to find answers, Killian retreated to his room, allowing the connection he shared with Ivy to guide him. He settled onto the floor, legs crossed, and closed his eyes.

Concentrating on the bond that linked their souls, he felt the familiar pull of her powers as they intertwined with his own.

"Father, I call upon you," Killian whispered into the darkness, feeling the energy surge through him. "Guide me to that fateful night."

As if in response, a rush of sensations flooded his senses – the smell of damp earth, the taste of blood on his tongue, the sound of distant screams echoing through the night. Like a storm raging within him, the memories threatened to tear him apart. But he held on, desperate for the truth.

"Show me," he pleaded, his voice barely audible as the world around him dissolved, giving way to the past.

In that instant, Killian was transported back to the night his father had died, his five-year-old self cowering in the shadows as chaos tore through the pack.

The scent of fear hung heavy in the air, accompanied by an underlying stench of something... darker.

Killian's vision swirled, shifting from the present to the past.

He felt his body shrink and his senses dull as he became his five-year-old self on that fateful night. The sounds of laughter and celebration filled the air as the pack revelled in the festivities.

"Killian, come join us!" a voice called out, beckoning him closer to the heart of the party. But his attention was drawn elsewhere – towards the hall where his father had disappeared earlier in the evening.

Curiosity piqued, young Killian cautiously approached the imposing wooden doors. The noise from the party receded into the background, replaced by an eerie silence that sent shivers down his spine. As he pushed open the doors, a sickening, metallic scent assaulted his nostrils – the stench of blood.

"Father?" he whispered, fear gripping his chest as he stepped further into the dimly lit hall. His eyes widened in horror at the sight before him – his father's lifeless body sprawled across the floor, crimson pooling around him. It was an image that would haunt his dreams for years to come.

The pack's reaction was visceral; cries of shock and grief echoed through the room as they rushed to their fallen leader's side.

But mixed in with their anguish, Killian could see that something wasn't right.

Was it the way some pack members exchanged nervous glances?

Or the lingering scent of dark magic that permeated the air?

"Get away from him!" one of the older wolves snarled at young Killian, his protective instincts kicking in.

Confused and frightened, Killian obeyed, retreating to the shadows where he could only watch helplessly as his world shattered around him.

As the years passed, Killian clung to that memory, desperate to find the answers that eluded him. Now, tapping into Ivy's power, he pushed himself further into the past, scouring every detail for clues about what had really happened that night.

But his relentless quest came at a steep price. The force of Ivy's magic surged through him, threatening to overwhelm his senses and drag him into the abyss.

His vision blurred, and he felt as if he were being pulled apart by an unseen force – one that threatened to claim him entirely.

"Stop... please..." Killian gasped, struggling against the darkness that sought to consume him. He knew he was overusing Ivy's power, but he couldn't let go – not when he was so close to finding the truth.

In that moment, on the brink of oblivion, Killian realized the cost of his obsession. And as the underworld's grip tightened around him, he mustered the strength to wrench himself free of its grasp.

Panting and drenched in cold sweat, Killian collapsed onto the floor, the echoes of his past still ringing in his ears.

As Killian lay gasping on the floor, his vision blurred and his body trembling from the force of Ivy's power that had nearly consumed him, Erin rushed to his side.

Her face etched with concern, she gently cupped his cheek, urging him back to the present.

"Killian, it's over now," Erin whispered, her voice a soothing balm against the cacophony of memories still echoing in his mind. "You're safe."

He blinked, focusing on the warmth of her touch and the softness of her eyes until the world stopped spinning around him. Erin leaned down, her forehead pressed against his as she held his gaze.

"Killian, you need to know that I've never taken our relationship lightly," Erin told him, her voice raw with emotion. "I will do whatever it takes to have you back, to help you through this."

Her words were the anchor he hadn't known he needed, pulling him back to reality. But as grateful as he was for her support, there was a tight, uncomfortable knot forming in his chest.

He thought of Ivy – her laughter, her strength, her unwavering belief in him – and realized, with a sinking feeling, that his heart belonged to Ivy despite Erin's reassurances.

"Erin, I..." Killian trailed off, unsure how to express the turmoil of emotions swirling within him. As his thoughts raced, a fragment of his recent flashback came into focus: the reflection of a muscular arm in the glass door, adorned with a tattoo of an unfamiliar symbol.

It wasn't from the pack – why had he never recalled that detail before?

"Killian?" Erin prompted, her eyes searching his face for answers. He took a deep breath, knowing he couldn't keep his feelings from her any longer.

"Erin, I appreciate everything you've done for me, but... my heart belongs to Ivy," he admitted, his voice heavy with regret. "I can't ignore that any longer."

The moment the words left his lips, Killian could see the hurt flicker across Erin's face, but she quickly masked it behind a practiced smile.

"Thank you for being honest with me," she said quietly, her tone laced with sadness. "I just want you to be happy, Killian."

Then she stood up and walked away, leaving him to his thoughts.

Killian tried to get more information from the vision of the tattooed arm from his mind. He knew it was a crucial piece to the puzzle of his father's death – one that could potentially change everything he thought he knew about that fateful night.

Killian's pulse raced, his mind fixated on the mysterious tattoo from his flashback.

He couldn't waste any time; he needed to share this new information with Ciaran.

"Viv!" Killian called out as he rounded a corner and nearly collided with her.

She jumped, surprise etched on her face.

As she turned to face him, Killian's breath hitched in

his throat – there, peeking out from beneath the strap of her tank top, was a familiar symbol inked into her skin.

"Hey, Killian," Viv said hesitantly, her green eyes wide with curiosity. "What's going on? You look like you've seen a ghost."

"Your tattoo. Where did you get that from?"

# ELEVEN

The sun dipped low, casting long shadows through the trees of the Sanctuary as Ivy stood in the clearing.

It took her an entire day to clear her head about what happened with Vincent before she felt that she was halfway ready to come here and face any questions Killian might ask. But once she was introduced to Erin, a new line of thought occupied her mind. Ivy couldn't quite figure out why, but there was something off about Erin. When Vincent talked about her, Ivy had pictured a different woman--not the formidable and beautiful one standing in front of her. She didn't look like the type who would submit to a husband's abuse.

The atmosphere was thick with tension, and she could feel it like a physical weight on her shoulders.

She tried to focus on the beauty of the woods—the way the leaves shimmered in the golden light, the whisper of a breeze rustling through the branches—but her gaze kept finding its way back to Erin.

Erin was the kind of woman who could make anyone feel inadequate: tall and slender, with long, raven hair that tumbled down her back in soft waves. Her eyes, an intense shade of blue, were framed by dark lashes that seemed to go on forever. She had a regal air about her, and even standing here amongst the dirt and foliage, she looked as if she belonged on the cover of a fashion magazine.

"Thank you for handling Vincent," Erin said, her voice smooth as honey, while Ivy felt as if hers would come out in a strangled croak.

"Of course," Ivy replied, trying to sound more at ease than she felt. "We're all in this together, right?"

Erin smiled warmly, but there was something in her eyes that made Ivy feel as if they were competing for something far more important than a place in Killian's pack. And Ivy knew, deep down, that if it came down to a choice between them, she wouldn't stand a chance.

"Can I talk to you for a moment?" Erin asked, her eyes flicking towards the others who were gathered nearby.

"Sure," Ivy said cautiously, following Erin to a more secluded spot within the trees.

As they walked, Ivy couldn't help but notice the grace in Erin's movements, the way she seemed to glide over the uneven ground. Ivy felt clumsy and awkward in comparison, her steps heavy and uncertain.

"I wanted to thank you," Erin said softly, her eyes shining with unshed tears. "For killing Vincent."

Ivy felt a jolt of surprise at the raw emotion in Erin's voice. It was hard to reconcile this vulnerable woman with the poised, sophisticated one she had been admiring just moments before.

"Erin... I'm so sorry you had to go through that," Ivy said, her own voice thick with emotion. "Nobody should ever have to suffer like you did."

"Thank you," Erin whispered, wiping away a tear that had managed to escape. "But I also need to thank you for something else."

"Wha—what's that?" Ivy asked, feeling a strange mixture of curiosity and dread.

"Killian," Erin said simply, her gaze locked onto Ivy's. "He's been so different since you came into his life. You've made him happy and I can see it. But I need you to know that I still care about him deeply."

Ivy swallowed hard, feeling as if her chest was being squeezed tight. She knew what Erin was saying without having to hear the words: Killian was hers.

"Erin, I—" Ivy started, but the words caught in her throat, choking her.

"Please don't take this the wrong way," Erin continued, her eyes filled with sincerity. "I just needed you to know how I feel. We all have our part to play in protecting each other, and I would never want to stand in the way of Killian's happiness."

Ivy took a deep breath, trying to push aside her emotions from the conversation with Erin. She couldn't afford to be distracted when there were more pressing matters at hand.

"I'm going to call Liam," she announced. "We need to know what's happening in the city and if there are any new threats."

"Put it on speaker, please" Killian said, his eyes never leaving Ivy's face, as if searching for some hidden meaning behind her words.

*Since when did he have to double-check the meanings of whatever she said?*

Ivy nodded, pulling out her phone and dialing Liam's number. As the call connected, she set the phone down on the table, activating the speaker function.

"Hey, Ivy," Liam greeted her, his voice tinny through the phone's speaker. "What's up?"

"Hey, Liam," Ivy replied, trying to sound casual. "We were hoping you could give us an update on the situation in the city. Have there been any new developments with the magical forces threatening our community?"

"Actually, yeah, there have been," Liam said, his tone growing serious. "There's a lot of paranormal activity around town, especially near the borders of your territory. It's like something is brewing, waiting for the right moment to strike."

"Anything specific we should be worried about?" Ciaran asked, leaning closer to the phone.

"Hard to say," Liam admitted. "But I've heard whispers that whatever is coming is powerful and won't be easy to stop."

"Thanks for the info, Liam," Ivy said, her heart pounding in her chest. "Keep us updated if anything else comes up."

"Will do," Liam promised before hanging up.

As Ivy pocketed her phone, Ciaran stood up abruptly and walked over to his laptop that was sitting on a nearby desk. He typed quickly, his fingers flying across the keyboard, and then beckoned Nina over.

"Look at this," Ciaran whispered to Nina, gesturing towards the screen. Ivy couldn't see what they were looking at, but she could sense the growing tension in the room.

Nina's eyes widened as she took in whatever information Ciaran had found. "This is bad," she said, her voice barely audible.

"Tell us what you found," Killian said.

"Based on my private connections and scans of supernatural activity," Ciaran began, his voice grim, "the highest level of paranormal pressure is converging over the city. It's like a storm waiting to break."

"Like Liam said," Ivy murmured, her thoughts racing with potential scenarios. "What are we up against?"

"Hard to say without more information," Ciaran admitted. "But one thing is clear: it has something to do with the Underworld."

The air in the room was thick with tension as Killian stepped forward, his brows furrowed.

"Demons?" Killian asked.

Ciaran nodded. "The true dark power."

"KILLIAN, maybe you should try talking to your father," Ivy suggested, "He might have some answers or guidance that could help us."

Killian hesitated, his jaw clenching. He had rarely summoned the spirit of his father since his death, but desperate times called for desperate measures.

With a deep breath, he closed his eyes and focused his energy inward.

"Father," he whispered, his voice strained with emotion. "I need your guidance."

A chill swept through the room as the air around them shimmered, and Ayden LeBlanc's spirit materialized before them. His eyes held centuries of wisdom, and they settled on Killian with a mixture of pride and concern.

Judging by Ciaran's expression, Ayden had made himself visible to everyone in the room.

"Father, we're facing an unknown enemy that threatens our pack, our family. We suspect it is the work of demons, but we don't know what they want from us," Killian explained, his voice wavering.

"Your territory has been protected by a powerful spell, cast by our ancestors to safeguard us from magical forces," Ayden said, his ethereal voice echoing throughout the room. "As long as you stay within its borders, and you'll be safe," said Ayden.

"So this is the work of the Underworld? Demons?" asked Ivy.

"Yes," he replied.

"Why now, and what do they want?" enquired Ciaran.

Ayden sighed. "I don't know the purpose behind this attack on our family. But the protective spell only takes effect if something nears our sacred ground."

"Where exactly is it, and what lies in it?" Killian wanted to know.

"It has been passed down through generations as a place of great importance. If someone dares to trespass its boundaries, they will face the full strength of the spell. Its location, however, I'm not aware of."

Ciaran paced back and forth around the room. "Is there any connection with our family's vault? Does this sacred ground pertain to both shifters and non-shifters?"

Ayden shook his head sadly. "If I had known that much, I could have saved myself from death. I don't know if the vault is real or not. But I believe the sacred ground existed prior to our family's division, thus implying that it concerns both sides."

"Remember, my son, you are never alone," Ayden said, his voice filled with love and pride. "Your family, your pack... they are your strength. And you, Ivy, your connection to the magical world is a gift. Use it wisely."

"What will happen if someone breaches the sacred ground?" Ivy asked.

Ayden hesitated for a moment before responding. "It would threaten the very existence of all shifters, as it would unleash a force from the magical world that we cannot control."

Ivy reached for a piece of chalk by the recipe board on the kitchen counter and began to draw.

"Does this white daisy with a single blue petal have any significance in all this?" Ivy questioned, holding up the picture of the peculiar flower.

Ayden's eyes widened and his transparent form flickered. "That... that is what killed me," he whispered, and then vanished without another word.

THE ROOM WAS LEFT in stunned silence, the weight of Ayden's revelation settling heavily upon them.

The sound of shuffling caught their attention as Vivian emerged from the shadows, rubbing her eyes sleepily.

She took one look at the drawing of the daisy in Ivy's hand and let out a string of profanity that belied her age.

"Where the hell did you find that damn thing?" Vivian demanded, her tattooed shoulder visible beneath her disheveled hair.

"Viv, what do you know about this flower?" Killian asked urgently, stepping closer to the girl.

"High-ranking members of my druid clan used something like that to make a potion," she explained, squinting at the daisy. "Helps 'em go into trances and travel to different worlds and shit. They can't grow the flowers themselves, though. Gotta pray for 'em or somethin'. There's always a price, or a sacrifice, involved."

Ivy's fingers clenched the chalk so tightly that it snapped.

"ALL RIGHT, EVERYONE," Killian said, his voice firm but calm. "We need to come up with a plan to protect the pack and find out what's going on with these magical forces."

"I'll cast more protective spells on the fences around the Sanctuary for immediate protection," Ivy declared. "The protective spells on the territory borders are great, but the Kyneton pack's territories span like half a continent; too large for the protection to be effective."

Killian chuckled. "No, we just own Mount Macedon ranges and a handful of regions around it. That's not half a continent. But yes, Ivy, more protective spells on our fence lines around the Sanctuary is an excellent idea."

As the group began to discuss their options, the front door burst open, revealing Fiona and Quinn, both panting heavily from their run.

Ivy's heart swelled at the sight of her adoptive mother, who immediately noticed the tension in the room.

"Did we miss something?" Fiona asked, her green eyes scanning the faces around her.

"Viv just told us about a dangerous flower connected to Ayden's death," Ivy explained briefly, not wanting to dive too deep into the complex situation.

Fiona's gaze landed on Viv, and her eyes narrowed as she spotted the tattoo on the young druid's shoulder. Without warning, Fiona shifted into her lynx form and charged at Vivian with a snarl.

"Mom!" Ivy yelled, panic seizing her chest. The room erupted into chaos as everyone scrambled to react.

"Shit!" Vivian cursed, dodging Fiona's attack by jumping onto a nearby table, knocking off plates and glasses in the process. She sprinted toward the back door, slipping out just as Fiona lunged for her again.

"Viv, no!" Ivy cried out, realizing that the girl hadn't heard the part about staying within the borders of the pack territory.

"Leave it to me," Ciaran said, already moving toward the door. He gave Killian a nod before disappearing after Vivian.

"Everyone else, stay put," Killian ordered, his eyes locked on the door through which Vivian had fled. "Ciaran can handle this. Vivian trusts him."

Ivy couldn't help but feel a pang of hurt at Killian's words. It was true that Vivian didn't seem to care for anyone with a demon connection, and Ivy couldn't deny the darkness that resided within her.

But she wished Killian had more faith in her ability to handle the situation.

"Let's focus on our plan," Killian continued, turning back to face the group. "We need to make sure everyone stays within the borders until we can figure out what's going on."

"Agreed," Nina chimed in. "We should also gather any information we can on these magical forces. The more we know, the better prepared we'll be to face them."

Damien rolled his eyes in exasperation. "Now we're stuck here. Our ancestors have constructed a prison for us in our own territory. This is fantastic!"

"Right," Ivy said, forcing herself to push aside her feelings of inadequacy. There was too much at stake for her to wallow in her own self-doubt.

She needed to be strong and resourceful, not just for herself, but for everyone who was depending on her.

As they continued to discuss their strategy, Ivy couldn't help but glance anxiously at the door, hoping that Ciaran would return soon, and praying that Vivian would be all right.

# TWELVE

Ivy leaned on a tree near the edge of the sanctuary, gazing at Damien as he practiced his newfound abilities. She couldn't help but feel a sense of pride watching him regain his strength and adapt to his new life as a werewolf.

Ivy knew how important Damien was to Nina, and seeing him grow into a potential leader brought her joy.

"Look at him, Ivy," Nina said, sidling up beside her. "He's come so far in such a short time."

"I know," Ivy agreed, a smile tugging at her lips. "Killian must be doing something right."

As if on cue, Killian stepped into the clearing, his strong form drawing Ivy's attention.

He approached Damien, an air of authority surrounding him. Ivy couldn't deny the magnetic pull she felt towards him, even from this distance.

"All right, Damien," Killian called out, clapping his hands together. "Time to work on controlling your shifts.

Remember what I taught you about focusing your energy."

Damien nodded, determination flashing in his eyes. He closed them briefly, taking a deep breath before his body began to tremble.

Ivy watched in awe as fur sprouted from his skin, his limbs contorting and reshaping until he stood on all fours as a magnificent wolf.

"Excellent!" Killian praised, stalking around Damien's wolf form. "Now, try shifting back."

Ivy observed the scene intently, her heart pounding in anticipation. Damien's transformation was nothing short of remarkable, and she found herself holding her breath as he attempted to shift back into his human form.

A low growl rumbled from deep within Damien's chest as he concentrated. His muscles tensed, and then, just as quickly as he had become a wolf, he shifted back into a man.

Ivy let out a relieved breath, her eyes never leaving the spectacle before her.

"Amazing," Nina whispered beside her, beaming with pride. "I knew he could do it."

"Indeed," Ivy agreed.

"Great job, Damien," Killian said, his voice full of genuine warmth as he clapped Damien on the back. "We'll keep practicing until you can shift seamlessly between forms. But for now, take a break."

"Thank you, Killian," Damien replied, fatigue evident in his voice but his eyes shining with gratitude.

As Ivy continued to watch the scene unfold, she

couldn't help but feel a surge of hope for the future. If they could harness the power of these extraordinary beings and work together, perhaps they stood a chance against the darkness that threatened their world.

IVY LEANED AGAINST A TREE, her arms crossed over her chest as she watched Erin work.

She didn't know why, but something about the woman rubbed her the wrong way.

Ivy's instincts were usually spot-on, and right now they were telling her to be cautious around Erin.

"Here, Damien," Erin said, holding out a small vial filled with a thick, green liquid. "Drink this. It will help you fully develop your abilities as a werewolf."

Ivy studied Erin's face, searching for any hint of deception. Erin's expression remained neutral, revealing nothing. Still, the unease in Ivy's gut persisted.

"Thank you," Damien said, taking the vial from Erin and downing its contents without hesitation.

Ivy clenched her fists, silently praying that her suspicions were unfounded.

"Erin's ability to compound natural potions for shifters is one of a kind," Killian remarked, his voice tinged with admiration. "She's been invaluable to our pack."

"Indeed," Ivy murmured, forcing herself to smile. She knew she couldn't let her personal feelings interfere with their mission. They had enough obstacles to overcome without adding unnecessary tension to the mix.

"Ugh, that tastes awful," Damien complained, making a face as he handed the empty vial back to Erin.

"Sorry," Erin replied, her lips curving into a small, apologetic smile. "But it's effective, I promise."

As Damien nodded, Ivy noticed the faintest glimmer of an unknown emotion in Erin's eyes – something that made Ivy's stomach clench with unease. But before she could examine it further, the moment passed, and Erin turned away to gather her potion-making supplies.

"Alright, everyone," Killian announced, clapping his hands together. "Let's get back to training.

"Right," Ivy said, pushing herself off the tree and moving to join the others. She cast one last wary glance at Erin before focusing her attention on the task at hand.

Inside the house, Ciaran stood outside Vivian's closed door, his hand hovering over the doorknob. He took a deep breath and knocked gently.

"Viv, it's Ciaran," he called out softly. "Can I come in?"

"Go away," came the muffled reply from within.

"Please, Vivian, we could use your help out here," Ciaran persisted, trying to keep his tone calm and reassuring.

"Leave me alone!" Vivian shouted back, her voice cracking with emotion.

Ciaran sighed, running a hand through his hair. He knew all too well how it felt to be young, scared, and misunderstood. He decided to take a different approach.

"I need help, Viv, come on!" he said, leaning against the doorframe. "I'm the only non-magical person here. I'm not a shifter. I don't do magic. If you won't help, I don't know what to do."

There was silence for a moment, and then the door cracked open just a bit. Vivian's eyes peeked out, red-rimmed and wary.

"What's your problem, Pretty Head, apart from the obvious?"

"I have many problems, Viv. But the main thing is, nobody here understands me."

"Really? Try me." The door opened a little wider, and Vivian stepped out into the hallway, wrapping her arms around herself protectively. "When I was five, I lost my dog, Dew, to a pack of wild dogs. I was so angry that I accidentally conjured a thunderbolt strike that devastated the entire hillside. I killed a lot of innocent animals in my rage, and I've regretted it ever since. I don't understand the power I have, and I can't control it. I still don't. So, sometimes people ask me for help, and I refuse because I know the consequences of what I do might be larger than they try to achieve. Then I'm blamed for being selfish. When I say I have no supernatural powers, those who have seen my thunderbolts would say that I lie or am being a coward."

"You're not a coward,"

"Neither are you. Sometimes..."

"I ran from lynx ... I mean Fiona. I almost crossed the boundary and almost dragged you outside the boundary too. You might have gotten eaten by the wolves. Aren't you mad at me?"

"No, of course I'm not mad at you. How could I be? Fiona was absolutely scary when she shifted. I would have run too if she attacked me.Plus, she didn't attack you. The tattoo you have on your shoulder is the daisy Fiona was afraid of. She was frightened of you, not the other way around.

"Are you sure?"

"Positive."

"It's just

"When I was little, I was abandoned in the woods by my family. I was attacked by lynx and dingos, and every time I see Fiona, I'm reminded of those horrible memories."

He looked down at her, his voice earnest. "Our abilities can be dangerous if we don't control them or use them for good. But you're a druid with so much potential, Viv. You can help the shifters, and not all lynx and shifters are bad, I promise."

Vivian bit her lip, considering Ciaran's words. Slowly, she nodded.

"Okay," she whispered, her eyes shining with unshed tears. "I'll try. How can I help?"

"Thank you, Vivian," Ciaran said warmly, placing a comforting hand on her shoulder. "We'll need a potion similar to that which your people make in order to cross realms, but we won't be using flowers as the main ingredient. Can you create it without them?"

"If I manage to make it, do you dare try it?"

Ciaran squinted at the young girl who was testing him. "If you can concoct it, I'll be your first guinea pig."

NINA, sensing Vivian's lingering unease, took Fiona gently by the arm and led her toward the far end of the sanctuary. Ivy watched with appreciation as Nina spoke softly to Fiona, her voice soothing like a gentle breeze rustling through leaves.

"Let's give Viv some space," Nina said, gesturing to the expanse around them. "This area is peaceful and will help her feel more comfortable."

Fiona nodded, understanding the need for distance between herself and the young druid. As they walked away, Ivy could see Vivian visibly relax, her shoulders dropping as if a heavy burden had been lifted from them.

With Fiona and Nina occupied, Ivy decided to patrol the borders of the sanctuary, her eyes scanning the surrounding area for potential threats. The sun cast long shadows across the ground, playing tricks on her eyes as she moved stealthily through the underbrush.

As Ivy rounded a bend in the path, her heart skipped a beat as she spotted Fiona and Nina approaching her, their expressions serious. Ivy's senses sharpened, ready for whatever news they had to share.

"Is everything alright?" Ivy asked.

"Everything's fine," Nina assured her. "We just wanted to check in and make sure things are secure here."

"Good," Ivy replied, nodding her head. "I haven't found any signs of trouble so far."

Just as the words left her lips, a sudden chill swept through the air, sending a shiver down Ivy's spine. She looked up, her breath catching in her throat as she saw Patrick's spirit materialize before her.

"Patrick," Ivy gasped, her heart pounding in her chest. "What...how?"

"Please, Ivy," Patrick pleaded, his spectral form shimmering in the fading light. "I need your help. I need to speak to Fiona and Nina." His eyes flicked toward his wife and daughter, who stood nearby, oblivious to his presence.

"Can't they see you?" Ivy whispered, glancing back at Fiona and Nina.

"No," Patrick replied, his expression pained. "I'm dead. Only you can see me because of your connection to the demon. Please, help me communicate with them."

Ivy said, shaking her head in disbelief. "I thought you weren't really dead."

Patrick sighed, the sound like a mournful whisper on the wind. "Unfortunately, I am. If I weren't, Fiona and Nina would be able to see me. I'm a new ghost. I don't have the power to pick and choose who I make myself visible to."

"I'll have to ask them if they want to speak to you. You didn't exactly give them a loving family; you talked to them, what, once a year? What do you want to say to them now?"

"I just want to say sorry to them. Only in death that I know how valuable family is to me."

Ivy chuckled. "Now, if this were in a novel I'd cry my eyes out and then do what you ask. But since I know you too well, I'm aware that being sentimental isn't your strong suit. So, give me one good reason why I should help you."

"I don't want Nina to take care for the mage business."

"That's what you wanted most in life. I don't believe you."

"No, I want the mage leadership. But, the leader in the round will go into the Trinity Witness consideration pool, and Nina is not meant to take that position."

"Then she shouldn't go for it."

"That's why I need to talk to her. Even if she doesn't try, if everyone else fails, then the position will fall on her lap."

"Isn't it a good thing?"

"No, because she'll be cursed."

"Come again."

Patrick growled. "That's the ultimate position everyone in the supernatural world wants."

"Not everyone, just the power hunger like you. But I get your point. Are you saying someone wants the position so badly and would curse everyone else who got to that position?"

"Yes."

"If that the post desirable position in the supernatural world, who would be in the position to curse the candidates? How can that even be possible?"

"I cursed Killian. It is possible."

Ivy stared at the flickering figure of Patrick.

"I placed the curse on Killian because he is a promising candidate. I'm not even active in the community. So, it is possible to curse a Trinity Witness candidate, I'm telling you."

"Can you hear yourself? You know I'm with Killian. And you are telling me that to ask me to help you? Are you insane or stupid?"

"I'm dead. What can you do to me? Kill me twice? But if you help me convince Nina to back down, then I'll give you the location of the potion to break the curse I have on Killian. it's in the Underworld. So, only dead people like me can get you there ..."

"How ..." before Ivy could complete her sentence another ghostly figure materialized in front of them. Killian's father, Ayden, appeared with fury in his translucent eyes.

"Patrick!" Ayden roared, his anger palpable. "You betrayed me for power and you cursed my son? We were like brothers!"

The air around them crackled with tension as Patrick hesitated, looking from Ivy to Ayden, his face a mix of guilt and defiance.

"Did you curse Quinn, too?"

"I ...," Patrick started, but before he could utter another word, Ayden lunged at him.

Ghosts collided mid-air, their translucent forms intertwining and clashing with a force that sent ripples through the atmosphere. The ground shook beneath Ivy's feet as she watched.

"Stop!" she shouted, but her plea went unheard amidst the chaotic cacophony of the ghostly battle.

Hearing the commotion, everyone rushed out from the sanctuary.

Ivy saw Killian and Vivian exchange worried glances, their eyes wide with shock as they witnessed the supernatural altercation.

The rest of the group could only see the destruction unfolding around them – trees uprooted, stones overturned, and debris flying – but not the ghosts themselves.

"Killian, what's happening?" Nina cried, fear etched onto her face as she clung to Fiona.

"Two ghosts are fighting," Ivy answered for him, her voice shaking. "Ayden and Patrick."

"Can we do anything to stop them?" Killian asked, his voice filled with concern as he looked helplessly at Ivy and Vivian, knowing they were the only other ones capable of seeing the spirits.

Ivy scanned the battlefield, her mind racing to find a solution. She felt torn between helping Patrick communicate with his family and protecting Killian from the very man who cursed him. But she couldn't risk letting this fight escalate further.

"Viv, can you use your druidic powers to calm them? Maybe create a barrier or something?" Ivy suggested, desperation creeping into her voice as she watched the two ghosts tear each other apart.

"I... I can try," Vivian stammered, clearly unsettled by the chaos around her. She closed her eyes and began to chant, her hands weaving intricate patterns in the air.

As Vivian's incantation grew in intensity, Ivy could feel the energy shifting. A soft, green glow emanated from the young druid, slowly expanding outward until it formed a barrier between the battling spirits.

The ghosts collided with the barrier, their anger momentarily subdued by the unfamiliar force. Ivy could see the confusion on their faces as they tried to comprehend what had happened.

"Enough!" Ivy yelled, "This fight solves nothing. We have bigger problems to deal with."

Silence fell over the group as they stared at Ivy, taking in the gravity of her words. The ghosts hesitated before backing away from one another, the tension between them still palpable but contained for now.

# THIRTEEN

The sharp scent of crushed pine needles filled the air as Ivy stood beside Killian, her gaze fixed on the raging spirits of Ayden and Patrick. Their translucent forms clashed amidst the woodland shadows, their ghostly faces twisted with fury. The Sanctuary, once a haven of peace, now trembled under the weight of their supernatural battle.

"Everyone," Ivy shouted above the howling wind, "just ignore them! We have more important things to deal with right now."

Killian nodded in agreement, his hand firmly gripping Ivy's for reassurance.

To their left, Vivian nervously chewed her lip, her eyes darting between the spirits and their friends.

Damien, Fiona, and Erin stared at the chaos unfolding around them, unable to see the ghosts but aware of their presence from the destruction they caused.

In that moment, Patrick's spirit suddenly appeared before Nina, snarling viciously.

A chill raced down Ivy's spine as she realized what was happening. "Nina, watch out!" she cried, but it was too late. With an unearthly shriek, Patrick lunged at Nina, his ghostly form tackling her to the ground.

"Help me!" Nina screamed, her voice laced with pain and terror.

Ivy felt her heart clench as she watched Patrick attempt to yank Nina's spirit from her body, his intentions clear: he wanted to take her to the underworld.

But how was it possible? Ivy had always believed spirits couldn't interact with the living like this.

"Viv, try something—anything to stop him!" Ivy commanded, her voice trembling with desperation.

As Ivy began chanting a spell, Viv followed suit, their voices rising in unison. But nothing happened. Patrick continued his assault on Nina, her cries growing weaker by the second.

"Please... stop..." Nina whimpered, tears streaming down her face.

"Damn it!" Ivy cursed, her hands shaking in frustration. "What do we do?"

"Keep trying," Killian urged. "We can't give up on her."

Ivy and Viv continued casting spells, their voices growing louder and more forceful.

But as the seconds ticked by, Patrick seemed only to grow stronger, his grip on Nina's spirit tightening as he prepared to drag her into the dark abyss of the underworld.

"Patrick, why are you doing this?" Ivy asked.

She continued casting spells alongside Killian and Vivian, but nothing seemed to have any effect on the ghost.

"Because I made a deal," Patrick snarled, his ghastly face twisted into a cruel grin. "I get one soul to take with me to the underworld. And I want my daughter!"

"Over my dead body!" Damien roared, his anger so intense he almost shifted into his wolf form. He and Ciaran moved quickly to support Nina's limp body, shielding her from the ravenous spirit.

"Enough!" Ciaran shouted, raising his hands in the air as he summoned a bolt of lightning.

The air crackled with energy, and with a flick of his wrist, the bolt shot towards a nearby tree. The tree erupted in a shower of sparks and splintered wood, toppling over and hurtling toward Patrick.

But the tree passed right through Patrick's spectral form, leaving him untouched.

"Damn it!" Ciaran cursed, his breathing ragged.

"Keep trying!" Ivy urged, beads of sweat forming on her brow.

The fight to save Nina consumed everyone's energy, their lungs burning and muscles screaming with exertion. As they continued their desperate struggle, Nina appeared to lose her grip on life, her breathing shallow and erratic.

"Please..." she whispered, her voice barely audible, "don't... let... go..."

Then, just when it seemed all hope was lost, Patrick

suddenly released Nina and lunged at Fiona, his ethereal fingers digging into her chest.

In a flash of otherworldly light, he disappeared, leaving his wife's lifeless body crumpled on the ground.

"Mom!" Nina sobbed, crawling toward Fiona's body, her strength depleted.

"Damien, help her," Ivy ordered, her voice hoarse with exhaustion.

"Fi... Fiona..." Killian murmured, his eyes filled with shock and grief.

"Patrick's target was Fiona the whole time," Viv whispered, her face pale.

"Come on," Ivy said, her own heart heavy with sorrow. "We need to regroup and figure out our next move. We can get her back"

But as they stared at Fiona's lifeless body, the weight of their exhaustion bearing down on them, the group couldn't muster the energy to give chase or do anything but stand there in numbed silence.

"HER BODY IS STILL WARM, I can bring her back. I won't stand here wallowing," Ivy declared as she paced the yard.

Killian locked eyes with her. "We can bring her back. We can see spirits and souls, we are experienced in combat. And I won't let you go anywhere alone, Ivy."

"The creatures down there will eat you alive! From what I heard, they're always hungry," Viv warned.

Ciaran shook his head. "We just need a careful plan: a

way in, and many ways to exit. I can arrange for a portal opening but I'll need an invitation from someone down there. I can usually arrange that, but it won't come quick."

"An invitation?" Damien asked, his brow furrowing as he glanced between Ivy and Ciaran. "How do we get one of those?"

"Leave that to me," Ivy replied, her eyes distant as she considered their options. "I have a few connections that might be able to help."

"You'll need a very good plan for what to do down there, too," Nina said.

"True," Killian agreed. "We'll need to cover ground fast, avoiding any unnecessary confrontations. We'll likely encounter lost souls and malevolent entities, so we'll need to be prepared for anything."

"Exactly," Ivy said, her gaze locked with Killian's. "We should gather our resources and weapons before we go. And don't forget about protection spells."

"Right," Ciaran added, a smirk appearing on his face. "I'll make some calls and arrange for a drop-off of weapons specifically designed for battling supernatural creatures. We'll also need silver blade daggers, as guns might not work in the Underworld."

"Sounds like we have a plan," Damien said, his voice a mix of determination and trepidation.

"Once the portal is open," Ivy warned, her eyes sweeping over the group, "there's no turning back. This will be dangerous, but we must succeed. For Fiona."

"Agreed," Killian replied, his face set in a grim expression. "Let's get to work."

Ivy's eyes scanned the yard, her mind racing with strategies and preparations. She knew she needed to call in a favor from an old ally who owed her one. With a deep breath, Ivy closed her eyes and spoke the incantation that would summon Lyrisa.

"Lyrisa, servant of Selene, hear my call. We require your aid."

A gust of wind swirled around them, scattering leaves and debris. As it settled, Lyrisa appeared – a vision of ethereal beauty with silver hair and delicate features.

"You can't go for a week without calling me, Ivy."

"I get quite attached to the supernatural these days. We need to retrieve Fiona's soul from the Underworld. We need and invitation to enter. Can you help us?"

"Ah, I see," Lyrisa said, her voice soft and tinged with sadness. "The Underworld is no place for the living, but I will grant your request. For old times' sake."

"Thank you, Lyrisa, we won't forget this."

Lyrisa smiled and raised her hands graciously. A parchment materialized before her, adorned with intricate symbols and celestial script.

She recited a litany in an ancient language, and as she finished, the parchment glowed with divine energy.

"This will grant you passage into the Underworld. Use it wisely, for I can offer no further assistance once you're there."

"Understood," Killian interjected, his voice firm. "We'll be cautious."

"See that you are," Lyrisa warned, her gaze flicking

from Ivy to Killian. "The Underworld is treacherous, and the dangers there are unlike any you've ever faced." With that final admonishment, she vanished as quickly as she'd appeared.

"All right," Ivy said, turning to Viv. "We're going to need a way to help Fiona's soul once we find her."

"On it."

Viv nodded, already gathering herbs and stones for a ritual.

"I can whip up some druidic bracelets for y'all. These will help make the journey between worlds easier, especially for Fiona's spirit returning to her body.

"Good," Killian replied, his eyes fixed on Viv as she prepared the ritual space. "The sooner we can get her back, the better."

Viv traced symbols on the ground, each line glowing with an unearthly light. She chanted words that seemed to resonate with the very air around them, and the wind picked up once more, whispering secrets long forgotten. As she continued, the herbs and stones began to weave themselves together, forming three delicate bracelets, each adorned with intricate patterns and powerful sigils.

"Take these," she said, handing one bracelet to Ivy and another to Killian. "When the time comes, place the third upon Fiona's spirit. The enchantments should guide her safely home."

"Thank you, Viv," Ivy said softly, fastening the bracelet around her wrist. It hummed with energy, pulsating against her skin like a heartbeat.

Ciaran paced back and forth, his fingers tapping against the screen of his phone as he made a series of calls. The tension in the air was thick, and Ivy watched him from the corner of her eye, taking notice of how his jaw clenched with each conversation.

"All right, I've arranged for some weapons to be dropped off by helicopter," Ciaran announced, pocketing his phone. "Guns might not work in the Underworld, but these silver-blade daggers should do the trick."

"You don't think we have knives?" Killian questioned.

Ciaran chuckled. "Not the kind I can supply."

"How long is the delivery going to take?" Damien asked.

Ciaran glanced at his watch. "I'd say, five minutes ago."

The hum of the helicopter reverberated in the air. A chopper flew over the front yard and a large package was dropped onto the grass.

Ciaran strode over, open the bag, selecting the blades in the bag."Against supernaturals, they're more reliable, I know you have powers and you both are experienced, but it's always best to be prepared." Ciaran explained, handing a dagger to Ivy.

She tested its weight in her hand, admiring the intricate engravings on the hilt.

"Thanks, Ciaran," Ivy said, slipping the dagger into a hidden pocket on her belt. "We appreciate it."

"Speaking of being prepared," Erin interjected, approaching the group with a small satchel in her hands. "I've brewed up some healing potions. They should help you recover from any injuries you might sustain."

"Thank you, Erin," Killian said gratefully, accepting the satchel. He opened it to find several vials filled with a shimmering blue liquid.

"Make sure you come back in one piece," Erin warned, her eyes filled with concern. "That's an order."

"Of course," Killian replied, touched by his friend's worry.

"All right, everyone," Viv spoke up. "Let's get these rituals started. This is the druid's way of doing this ..."

The group gathered in a circle, each member holding a different item: a candle, an herb, a crystal.

Ciaran smiled at Killian and Ivy. "What she means is her incantation will help to facilitate the process. You remember we did this before in London, don't you Ivy?"

"Yes, we went to the Between World for Ciaran."

"That's right, so with this trip, the basics are still the same; I use tech to detect possible points of entry between worlds. But there are a few changes to keep in mind. Firstly, my people can't be here, so they're doing this remotely. Secondly, as we have to stay here, I'm actively forcing the gateway's location instead of waiting for it to appear naturally. The good news is that the invitation we're using now is stronger than last time. Viv's incantation should help make the transition smoother on a supernatural level when we force our way through."

"What if they refuse us entry?" Killian asked.

"The Underworld isn't owned by anyone so rejecting us isn't an option. If we try to breach a particularly thick veil then it'll take much longer for the gateway to open but once inside...well, that's a different story altogether. Creatures in those realms have their own territories and interests to defend so that's where all your skills in both combat and negotiation come into play."

"Understood," Killian nodded.

Ciaran drew a round talisman from his pocket. It glowed a light blue hue in his hand. "Don't worry, I don't do magic... yet. But this is an offer that you can make; if they take this, then you'll get what you want without having to lift a finger or slitting throats."

He handed the item to Ivy. "In the Underworld, it's more likely that they'd rather talk to Ivy than you, Killian. So, you'll have her back and keep things on the right track, but let her make the deal."

Killian's lips curled into a snarl of objection, but then as if he thought better of it, he nodded.

"Repeat after me," Viv instructed, her voice clear and strong. "Aid us now in our quest, mighty spirits of the realms."

"Gairid sinn anois sa bhfios-searc, spioraid móra na réimsí," the group echoed.

Viv continued:

"Bíodh slánú ar ár gcairde trí na scáil, agus treoraidh siad chun bua.

Tá siad lucht leanúna agam ach thabhair iad abhaile go slán, le cosaint an misean acu críochnaithe agus comhsheasmhacht a n-nósanna a chomhthuigint."

. . .

As they finished reciting the incantation in Celtic, the air around them shimmered and sparked.

Killian and Ivy were wrapped in a cocoon of magic.

The gateway started to open.

The air crackled with energy, and a dark, swirling vortex appeared before them, its edges flickering like the flames of a dying fire.

"Are you ready?" Killian asked.

He gripped his silver blade tightly, the weapon glinting ominously in the dim light.

Ivy swallowed hard and nodded, her own dagger reassuring in her hand. "As ready as I'll ever be."

"Remember," Ciaran warned, his voice tense, "the portal will only remain open for a limited time. So do what you do need and return as quickly as possible."

"Understood," Killian said, clapping a firm hand on Ciaran's shoulder. "We'll make it back in time. I promise."

With Killian by her side, Ivy walked toward the swirling darkness before them.

The sensation was unlike anything Ivy had ever experienced - as if her very essence was being torn apart and reassembled in the blink of an eye. Then, as suddenly as it had begun, the feeling vanished, and she stumbled forward, her vision momentarily blurred.

"We're in!"

"Are you all right?" Killian's strong hand gripped her arm, steadying her as she blinked away the disorientation.

"Yes, you?"

"Yes."

Ahead of them lay a deathly black cavern, and the putrid stench of fresh carnage combined with a scent of brimstone threatened to overwhelm them. This was a portal to the supernatural underworld—a place of unspeakable darkness and horror.

# FOURTEEN

The stench of sulfur and decay assaulted Ivy's senses as she and Killian descended into the underworld. Shadowy creatures skulked in the gloom, red eyes glowing with malice. The twisting tunnels seemed to shift and change with every step, an endless maze designed to trap unwary souls.

Ivy gripped her dagger tight, magic crackling at her fingertips. "The soul depository should be this way."

Killian's fingers grazed the hilt of his dagger as he cautiously surveyed the murky tunnels.

"It's remarkable that your tarot cards can lead us down here," he uttered.

"I think this is where they were crafted! It feels like coming home for them!"

"Fascinating!"

The soul depository loomed before them, carved from obsidian and bone. Inside, souls floated in orbs of sickly green light, stored on massive shelves.

A soul reaper in a dark robe sat behind a desk, arguing with a smug-looking Patrick.

Ivy's nails dug into her palm. That bastard. He had no right to Fiona's soul. She started forward, magic flaring, but Killian caught her arm.

"Wait," he murmured. "We must be cautious." His golden eyes were hard as flint. "There may yet be a way to reclaim her soul without violence."

Ivy took a deep breath, reigning in her power. Killian was right. They had to be smart about this.

The soul reaper shook his head at Patrick. "The agreement was to end the woman's life so her soul could be collected. The soul is my fee. If you take the soul, it's like I'm working for you for free, and I don't do charity work."

"There is no charity here. Compassion isn't something a soul reaper possesses," Patrick retorted.

"Neither do greedy souls of untalented mages. Remember, I keep all your precious possessions in this depository. One wrong move and I'll destroy everything you've worked for in your pitiful life. No one in this realm will want to deal with you."

"The scheming scoundrel utilizes this depository as a Swiss bank of the underworld," Killian muttered. "That could play to our favor."

"Agreed," Ivy said.

Patrick's lips curled into a sneer. "You'll give me the soul, or you'll find those tunnels overrun with abominations."

"Don't you dare threaten me. You're a dead mage with no bargaining power," the soul reaper snarled.

"There's no need for threats." Ivy's voice echoed through the depository. "We've come to reclaim what is ours."

Patrick's eyes widened, and he took a step back. "You're here ... You—you're dead!"

Ivy arched a brow. "Death is relative. Now, will you give us Fiona's soul freely, or must I pry it from your cold, dead hands?"

A bead of sweat rolled down Patrick's temple.

Ivy smiled, sharp and predatory, her magic sparking at her fingertips. After everything he had done, it would be a pleasure to destroy him.

KILLIAN KEPT his hand on his dagger, eyes scanning the room for threats while Ivy dealt with Patrick.

The soul reaper was clearly unhappy with the situation, but seemed disinclined to interfere.

For now.

Ivy took a menacing step toward Patrick, magic flickering around her. "Well?"

Patrick's eyes darted around the room, no doubt seeking an escape. Finding none, he sagged in defeat. "Take the soul. Just leave me be."

Ivy smiled.

The room was filled with tension as the soul reaper smirked at Ivy's demand. Killian chimed in, adding more fuel to the fire.

"Sorry, Ivy. Patrick can't give you something he

doesn't have. Looks like we'll have to make a deal with the real owner of Fiona's soul."

Patrick refused to back down. "Fiona's soul belongs to me! We made an agreement!" he glared at the soul reaper.

The soul reaper leaned back in his chair.

"This depository is mine, and he was just another customer. You want anything here, you talk to me."

Patrick sprung up to his feet. "You can't do this!"

The soul reaper cast a glance at Patrick, then his attention returned to Ivy and Killian. "So, what do you offer for the soul in question?"

Ivy held up the talisman Ciaran had given her. The soul reaper approached, gazing upon the blue-glowing surface of the device. The brief instructions Ciaran had given them didn't make much sense before, but it was clear to Ivy now.

Depending on who looked at the talisman, it would detect their most desirable price and reveal what Ciaran's network could offer.

The soul reaper's eyes widened as he read. "Prepaid unconditional contracts with cross-world mercenaries, one soul per contract? Are you serious?"

Ivy squared her shoulders. "Do you think we'd walk on your turf and fake an offer?"

"No, you wouldn't dare. So, how many contracts will you trade for this soul in question?"

"It's Fiona's soul."

"Yes, Fiona's soul." He rolled his eyes.

Ivy glanced at Killian then back at the soul reaper."Five," Ivy answered confidently.

"Twenty," the soul reaper countered.

"Ten," Ivy countered back.

The soul reaper's eyes sparked with delight as he saw what seemed like a good deal to him.

"You greedy scum ..." Patrick snarled and charged at the soul reaper. The soul reaper swung his arms in the air and Patrick's soul was blasted with blackened fire; whatever remained of his existence exploded.

Ivy didn't know what sort of magic that was, but she knew this was truly the end of him.

"Bring us Fiona's soul," Ivy said.

The reaper scowled but nodded. He shuffled over to a shelf and retrieved a glowing orb—Fiona's soul.

Ivy's eyes softened at the sight of it, a surge of warmth and love and grief twisting in her chest.

The soul reaper held the orb in one hand and extended the other. "Give me thy talisman, now!"

Killian shifted, sheathing his dagger and wrapping an arm around Ivy in silent support.

"How do we know that this exchange is legitimate and that we can restore the soul to its bodily vessel?" Ivy queried.

The soul reaper sighed. "All right. I'll put it back right here, but then you will have to take her body back to your world yourself."

"That can be arranged," Killian said.

The soul reaper mumbled a spell. Fiona's body appeared on the ground. He raised his hand and slammed the orb of soul back into the body. Fiona gasped and sat back up on the ground, panting.

Ivy rushed over. "Mom, are you okay?"

Fiona was still disoriented.

"Mom, can you say something so that I know it's really you?"

"Wh ... what .. what's going on?"

Killian walked over. "Fiona, what's Ivy's favorite food?"

"My homemade potato and leek stew."

Ivy wiped a tear from her face. "That's her."

"Okay, let's get you out of here."

Killian helped Fiona stand up.

The soul reaper cleared his throat and reached his hand out again for the talisman.

"We're not done, yet," Ivy declared.

"What!" The soul reaper snarled.

"Ivy!" Killian stepped closer to her, ready to protect her if the reaper chose to lunge at her. Ivy held up a hand, signaling for Killian to know that she was in control of the situation.

"I can upgrade the offer," Ivy said confidently.

The soul reaper narrowed his eyes, suspiciously sizing up her proposal. "What do you have in mind?"

"You said before that you keep all of Patrick's precious possessions."

"That's true. No-one here is willing to deal with him."

"All right, then in Patrick's possession, there will be a jar of potion. I want that and can upgrade the offer to pay. You will have to check if you have that potion or not."

The soul reaper nodded and disappeared into the depths of the underworld.

Killian glanced at Ivy, understanding why she was asking for his only hope of breaking the curse upon him.

Moments later, the soul reaper returned with a heavy metal box and cast a spell to open it. Inside was a small jar of amber liquid that glimmered in the faint light.

The soul reaper picked it up and inspected its contents. "Is this what you want?"

Ivy nodded.

He shrugged. "All right. I want five contracts extra for this." He handed the potion jar over.

Ivy frowned. "What kind of potion is this?"

The soul reaper arched an eyebrow. "You don't know what you're trading for?"

"I know what I want. But I'm not sure if Patrick has it. He lied all the time. You know...."

The soul reaper glanced at the jar. "This is some kind of a curse breaking potion. The kind of cruse that mages like him conjured and cast on people. So, if you're after this to break some kind of curse, then it's a real deal. But, it's useless if the potion is not designed for a person."

"What do you mean?"

"Someone has to do something to tell this potion which curse it is breaking. Or you will be wasting it. And for that extra information, I want another five contracts."

"Do you know who can complete the potion?"

"No. Do you want it or not?"

"Yes." She took the potion and gave the soul reaper the talisman.

A bone-chilling shriek echoed through the room, the sound of rending stone and shattering glass following after. The tunnels were collapsing, walls cracking and crumbling as a horde of misshapen creatures flooded inside.

"Abominations! Foul creatures. I'm done here; get out!"

In a sudden burst of energy, Ivy, Killian and Fiona were quickly expelled from the depository.

"Run, quick!" Killian shouted.

They sprinted with all their might, widening the distance between them and the dismal horde.

As they kept running, the exit seemed closer and eventually, the cacophony of the creatures had lessened to silence.

THEY MADE their way through the twisting tunnels, shadows flickering across the rough-hewn walls. An uneasy quiet had descended over the realm, as if the denizens were holding their breath in anticipation of the next attack.

Killian kept a wary eye out, one hand resting on the hilt of his dagger. "It's too quiet. Something isn't right."

"I feel it too," Ivy said. The hairs on the back of her neck prickled with every step.

"Is that the exit?" Fiona pointed toward the glimpse of the light.

"Yes, but this is too quiet, the exit might be an illusion or a trap," Killian said.

"No, that's a real exit. But not for you, wolf."

Ivy and Killian whirled around toward the voice.

From the shadow stepped out an oversized demon with bulging red eyes and razor sharp teeth stretched across a wide mouth. It had four horns protruding from its head and long claws extending from its hands. Its scaly skin was a deep black shade, and it towered over them menacingly.

"I'd urge you to think twice before you run."

"Don't turn your back on a demon, that much I know. What did I do to offend you?" Killian asked.

"You did nothing wrong. But Patrick has previously struck a deal with our protection services for ultimate protection while he is here."

"Well, he's dead, and your service failed. That has nothing to do with us," Ivy said.

"Yes, it does. Before his demise, he had already used our services but never got around to pay for them. In our agreement, if he can't cover the cost himself, the debt will be transferred to his successor and he specifically named you, Ivy. Though we don't want you, as for the payment currency of our services, we use hell hounds, and the best kind of hell hounds is the shapeshifter. So, we'll take Killian instead."

"That's utterly preposterous!" Ivy barked out; her hands were firmly grasping the hilt of her dagger.

Killian touched her hand on the dagger. "There must be something else that you want. I'm only a wolf shifter, and I can't shift at the moment. Surely I'm not as valuable to you as you might think."

The demon chuckled. "Oh, you are. If we don't take you, we'll take your pack. We have an evaluator in the house who told us how powerful you would be with the right training - after we turn you into a hell hound, of course."

"Go to hell," Ivy snarled.

"We're already at home, darling!"

Killian shook his head. "I won't work for you. I'll fight you to the death, so you will only lose if you try to keep me."

The demon growled.

"Growling isn't going to do you any good. Killian won't work for you, no matter how much you push us. It'll only cause you more issues and losses."

"I'm aware of what I'm doing; don't sass me. Even if Selene has a deal with you, it can't protect you here. She can't do as much as she thinks," the demon sneered.

"What deal?" Killian questioned, confusion contorting his face.

Ivy stepped forward towards the demon. "There is no deal with Selene; but there is a powerful connection between us, and you know that's true."

The demon paused briefly, agitation evident in their body language. Ivy knew she'd struck a nerve. "So, let me make it up to you by using my own power to do something for you."

The demon paced back and forth for a few moments before speaking again. "Yes, if you do one thing for me, then we'll be even."

# CHAPTER
# FIFTEEN

The acrid stench of sulfur filled the air, and Ivy's throat was ablaze with its harshness.

Behind them the landscape was a desolate wasteland, the land marred by jagged obsidian rocks and seething pools of lava. And above it all was an oppressive sky, a hellish red hue that seemed to stretch endlessly.

It was a hunter's paradise, countless hellhounds prowling the rocky terrain and stalking their prey.

Nowhere else could she hear such a cacophony of snarls and barks rising up from the depths below.

In front of them was the looming entrance of an old and desolate hell jail. The towering stone walls were encrusted with ivy, and their façade was blotted by decades of mold and grime. The metal gate hung crookedly from its hinges, giving off a loud creaking sound as it swayed in the chilly wind. In the silence of the night, the prison seemed to be scowling at them menacingly.

"It's a good thing that we sent Fiona back to the

Sanctuary with your potion. She hates jails, let alone a prison in hell. Your potion could be a treasure for those souls locked up in here. I'm sure they must be under some kind of curse," Ivy said.

"Not having to worry about Fiona is a relief. We'll have to get in and out of here quick," Killian muttered.

"That's the plan."

"We still have to talk about the deal you made with Selene without my knowledge, Ivy," Killian replied.

"Well, now is not the time, Killian."

"I'm not pleased that you agreed to this mission. The demon wanted me, not you. You could have returned with Fiona and sought help. We'll need to discuss this further when this is over. Establishing some regulations and protocols is essential for running an efficient pack. You can't go without rules..."

She pushed him against the wall and kissed him. She was usually aroused even by the tone of his voice. But now, it was more than physical attraction. She needed him like she needed air: an assurance of life.

And she knew he needed the same.

Killian only spoke this way when he was afraid, and that fear was now contagious. She knew she should keep her wits about her before embarking on such a dangerous mission--breaking out a bunch of reckless souls from their captors' stronghold--but all she could do was cling to Killian and hope he'd give her the strength to succeed.

"Are you pleased now?"

"Ivy..."

She kissed him one more time, and savored the taste

of him on her lips. "Let's do this. If you have any complaints, we'll discuss when this is over."

"Do this? You mean right here? Right now? ...."

She pecked his cheek. "I mean the mission. As for the pleasure activities, we can roam the sheets at the Sanctuary."

"Right, of course. This mission should be quick. It's difficult to put these creatures in jail, but breaking them out shouldn't be a problem. All we need to do is open the gate and they will take care of the rest."

She grinned. "See, we're on the same page on this."

He smiled, but the smile didn't reach his striking blue eyes.

Ivy delicately handled the tarot cards, inquiring about the location of the entrapped souls they needed to liberate. The cards shimmered and multiple arcane signs were revealed, pointing to the secret dungeon where the souls were caged.

They went through the twisting passages of the underworld, heading deeper into prison. The air grew colder and darker, shadows clinging to their heels with every step.

Killian's hand found hers, twining their fingers together. She gripped him tighter, drawing strength from his presence at her side.

After what seemed like hours of walking, they arrived at a massive iron gate. Beyond it was a vast, empty chamber—a perfect space to contain the most dangerous souls.

Ivy placed her hands on the cold bars, feeling the ancient magic woven through the metal. This gate marked the boundary between oblivion and a realm of pure nothingness. Any soul trapped there would cease to exist, obliterated from the cycle of life and death.

It was a fate worse than Hell.

Ivy took a deep breath and summoned her magic. It began to tingle and pulse, pulsing with each thud of her heartbeat. She poured it into the gate, which began to glow with silver light.

In a flash of light and energy, the bars burst open and exploded into a million tiny particles that swirled in the air like glitter.

The hundreds of forgotten souls, who had been languishing in the prison for an eternity, now unleashed from their shackles, surged out through the gates like a blazing torrent of flame, their anguished cries reverberating in the night air.

The souls burst out from their prison in a frenzied dance of liberation. Their faces were twisted with relief, and they let out cries of joy and triumph that echoed across the landscape, each step another celebration.

Some spun in circles, others leaped for joy, and a few knelt to kiss the earth.

As they reveled in their newfound freedom, the wind carried their laughter and shouts into the horizon. It was as if all of their pent up energy could finally be unleashed in a rush of uninhibited emotion.

The sound of the souls' murmurs slowly died down, and one by one, they left the prison walls. Ivy watched in awe as some floated toward her and bowed their heads in thanks. She was taken aback when she heard them murmur her name—she had no idea they could even speak. It was almost as if they knew who she was and were thanking her for liberating them.

"I believe this is the final group. We completed what we set out to do. The demons should be pleased now. Let's go, Killian."

Before they could leave, a bloodcurdling howl rang out, followed by the sound of snapping jaws and scraping claws.

Ivy and Killian froze in their tracks, swiveling to find the source of the commotion.

A massive black hound burst from the underbrush, its eyes glowing a demonic red. It let out an unnerving howl and was followed in short order by two more dogs of the same breed and temperament.

Then a whole pack charged straight for the exit, snarling and snapping at anything or their way.

"Hell hounds!" Ivy cried.

"They must have been locked in the same cell with the lost souls. Can you lock the gate?" Killian asked.

"No, I don't believe so."

Suddenly a large wall collapsed, and a horde of hell hounds spilled out.

They were huge beasts with razor-sharp claws and teeth, snarling and howling as they raced out into the night.

"The demon didn't mention anything about these monsters! This was not part of the deal!" Ivy screamed as Killian yanked her away from the impending attack.

"We need to go, right now, Ivy."

"We have to stop them before they reach the human world!"

"There are too many of them."

Panic and determination warred within her as Ivy summoned her magic once more. She had already given so much, but there was no other choice.

Gritting her teeth, Ivy flung a blast of power toward the leading hound.

The beast yelped as it was thrown backward, but the others continued their advance without faltering.

Ivy faced off against the snarling beasts, attacking with a vicious barrage of spells and curses. No sooner fell one hound than two more lurched from the underbrush, an unending wave of death that threatened to swallow them whole.

Her bones screamed for rest, but she pushed on through sheer force of will.

The world seemed to spin around her as the beast moved with lightning speed towards Killian.

The ground shook beneath them as he hit the dirt, its teeth glowing in the failing light as it pounced on his neck, rage and hunger flashing in its eyes like a wildfire. Its jaws opened wide to tear into his flesh, leaving no mercy behind.

Time seemed to stand still. A series of images flashed before her eyes; a life without Killian in it filled her with dread that settled over her like a dense fog. Her heart raced, and her stomach lurched as if she were falling.

She raised a hand, pulling forth all the power she had learned from the deities, dark magic, light magic--even what Patrick had taught her. With a guttural scream that echoed through the forest, Ivy unleashed an explosive beam of raw energy at the hound.

The force of it was enough to uproot trees and shatter boulders as it tore through the air like a fiery comet. The hound never stood a chance against Ivy's wrathful onslaught; in a flash of white-hot power, it disintegrated into ash that scattered across the clearing like black snowflakes.

Killian sprang to his feet, eyes fueled with rage. "You should have let me handle that one."

"You're welcome, Killian!" Ivy shouted back.

"Don't handle me, Ivy."

"We can talk about this later."

"If there is a later. At this rate we won't make it out alive even if we kill every last hound!"

There had to be a better way, Ivy thought. Some strategy that would turn the tide in their favor.

The answer came in a flash of inspiration.

Of course—why hadn't she thought of it sooner?

"Killian, get to higher ground!" Ivy ordered. "I have an idea."

He gave her a wary look but did as asked, scrambling up the rocky slope nearby.

Ivy took a deep breath and lifted her hands, drawing the power within her to the surface.

The ground began to shake and heave under Ivy's feet. Her eyes widened as she watched in horror as the earth started to crack, fissures forming at a rapid pace, and racing towards the pack of hell hounds.

The beasts yelped in alarm but it was too late—the gaping chasm opened beneath them, dragging the hounds down into the endless dark.

They plummeted into the seemingly infinite abyss,

their cries penetrating the darkness like a hammer striking steel. Ivy strained her ears to hear them echoing through the graveyard of crevices and craters that lined its murky walls.

Ivy gritted her teeth against the strain, feeling the weight of the world on her shoulders as she forced the fissure wider and deeper until the last hound's cries faded into oblivion.

She could feel every muscle in her body tensing, every sinew straining with effort as she willed more power into the fissure, making it wider and deeper still.

At last, the tremors stopped and Ivy sank to her knees, panting with exhaustion. The only sounds that remained were her own ragged breaths and the echo of distant snarls from below.

With the threat gone, she released the spell and collapsed to her knees, chest heaving.

Ivy sank to the ground, utterly depleted. Using that much magic had drained her nearly dry. She could barely lift her head as Killian slid down the rocky slope to join her.

As he pulled her into his arms, her whole body felt limp and lifeless, her magic dimmed to a flicker.

Killian scooped her into his arms. "There will be be more hounds coming out, I'm sure of it. Unless we can close the prison, but I don't know how and you have nothing left in you. I'm taking you back to the Sanctuary."

Too tired to argue, Ivy let her head droop against his chest.

KILLIAN CRUSHED IVY TO HIM, his powerful arms squeezing her until she felt as if she'd disappear into him.

His heart beat against hers like a barrage of drums, and the warm air of his breath sent goosebumps up her spine. Despite exhaustion pulling her under, Ivy couldn't help but feel alive in Killian's embrace.

They passed through the barrier between realms, leaving the underworld behind them.

She felt too blissful in his hold to worry about what was ahead of them; all she wanted was to savor this moment with him—the feeling of being securely held by the one man who could protect her from anything.

Even if it didn't last forever, this moment was her treasure to keep. Forever.

# SIXTEEN

Ivy's heavy eyelids slowly creaked open, an intense headache pounding in her head. She inhaled deeply and squinted toward the couch.

Killian lay on his back, his arms flung wide in a position of surrender. The light that filtered through the window cast light and shadow over the sharp angles of his face. With his shirt open to reveal taut muscles along his chest and stomach, he could have been a statue made by gods rather than a man carved from the earth. His skin was smooth as silk, full of life and energy.

His body mended rapidly when he rested. She had witnessed him recover from near-fatal injuries just by taking a break. The physiology of a shifter was remarkable.

"Good, you're awake," Nina said softly, appearing by Ivy's side with a warm smile. "How are you feeling?"

"Like I've been hit by a truck," Ivy murmured, sitting up gingerly.

"Uncle Finn and Damien managed to drive the hell

hounds back into the mountains," Nina explained, her hands wringing together nervously. "But it's only a temporary solution."

Ivy sat right up as the memories from the Underworld flooded back into her mind.

"I'm at the Sanctuary. In the human world. Did you just say something about hell hounds?"

The howling of the hell hounds echoed in the distance, making Ivy shudder involuntarily. The sound sent chills down her spine, reminding her of the danger that still loomed over them all.

Nina nodded. "Ciaran kept the gateway open waiting for you and Killian. But before you came back, a herd of hell hounds stormed out from that. Lucky that the portal was far outside the fence line of the Sanctuary, and the hounds seemed to bounce back from the protective spells you cast on the fences. Uncle Finn said the fence around our territory kept them from entering the human world. But those spells were cast ages ago, and he doesn't know how long they will hold."

Ciaran strode into the room, his brow furrowed in concern. He stopped by Ivy's bed, looking her over before turning his attention to Killian.

"You two are lucky," he said, his voice laced with relief. "Your injuries aren't too severe. You can heal yourself. Killian is almost done with his self healing process."

Killian stirred, then sat up on the sofa. His gaze shot to Ivy first. Seeing that she had been up and appeared fine, he exhaled, raking his hands through his hair.

"However," Ciaran continued, his tone growing more serious, "we need to address the hell hounds problem."

"You sound like you have a solution, Ciaran," Ivy said.

"Mercenaries," Ciaran suggested, his eyes flicking between Ivy and Killian. "We need skilled fighters from outside our territories to help us."

Killian shook his head, his protective instincts flaring. "I don't like it," he growled. "Bringing in outsiders could put us all at risk."

"Killian, we don't have much choice," Ivy interjected, her voice soft but firm. "We need help. We can't keep these hounds contained forever."

His jaw clenched, Killian reluctantly nodded. "Fine. But be careful who you bring in, Ciaran."

"Of course," Ciaran agreed, "I'll only use the best of the best."

As Ciaran left to make arrangements, Ivy glanced back at Killian.

"I'm going to speak with the demon. They must take responsibility for bringing the hounds back to the Underworld since this was not part of our agreement."

"I don't think we're ready to return there, Ivy. We barely escaped the hounds last night. They may be in the mountains now, but they could be right up against our fence in a flash. Creating a portal inside our fence is out of the question. We don't know what will escape from Hell this time."

***

. . .

CIARAN'S FINGERS danced over the keys of his laptop, the rapid clicking filling the room as he worked to find mercenaries willing to take on the hell hounds.

Ivy paced back and forth, her heart pounding in her chest as she listened to the distant howls echoing through the mountains.

"Got one," Ciaran announced triumphantly after what felt like an eternity. "They initially refused, but when I doubled the offer, they agreed."

Ivy exhaled, both relieved and apprehensive. Bringing outsiders into their world was risky, but it seemed there was no other choice. "When will they arrive?" she asked, her voice tense.

"Tonight," Ciaran replied, glancing at his watch. "They're flying in with choppers and weapons, but they need someone from the inside to guide them."

"Absolutely not, Ciaran" Killian growled from where he sat, still recovering from his injuries. "You, Nina, and Viv are staying put. You're not shifters. We can't afford a scratch on you from the hell hounds."

Damien stepped forward, his expression determined. "I'll go," he volunteered. "I can fight in human form and communicate with the mercenaries. And I think my body can heal like yours if I get bitten, right?"

Killian hesitated, clearly torn between wanting to protect Damien and recognizing that they needed all the help they could get. Finally, he nodded. "Be careful, Damien."

"Always am," Damien replied with a grin.

Nina hadn't said a word in the last ten minutes. She quickly ran across the room and reached up to Damien, her petite five foot frame struggling against his six foot two figure, before she planted a kiss on his lips.

Ivy could tell it was their first kiss; such ardor could have set the Sanctuary ablaze if they weren't careful.

Nina slipped a necklace with a lucky charm around his neck, pecked his cheek, and then released him.

After seeing Damien off, Nina returned to the house. Her eyes darted toward the corner where her pets were gathered.

"Where's Simba?"

Simba the cat wasn't with the Cavoodle Snuggle-worth and the husky Pixy. The two dogs looked at Nina with puppy eyes.

"Oh my gosh, did he follow Damien?"

Viv sat cross-legged next to the fireplace. "I saw him sneaking out after Damien. He's always jealous of the dogs. You said the dogs have supernatural talents, and Simba doesn't."

"He's just a cat. Nothing wrong with that."

"Well, he might want to hone some skills to compare to your supernatural ensemble."

Nina groaned and gave herself a face palm.

***

THE CHOPPERS DESCENDED upon the mountains, their blades slicing through the air like the grim reapers' scythes.

Damien met the mercenaries, their hardened expressions speaking volumes about their experiences in combat.

Together, they ventured into the treacherous terrain, armed to the teeth and ready for battle.

Damien wondered if the mercenaries knew they were fighting hellhounds and not just big dogs. But then, mercenaries are hire killers. They would kill anything that the contract specified. Ciaran paid top dollar. So these guys would sell their souls for this sort of money.

"That way," Damien pointed.

"Stay back, don't get in our way," a mercenary said.

Damien rolled his eyes on the inside. They treated him like a mere civilian.

As they encountered the first wave of hell hounds, the air filled with the sound of gunfire and guttural snarls. The mercenaries fought with ruthless efficiency, their bullets tearing through the monstrous creatures.

He couldn't help but feel a pang of sympathy for the hellhounds.

Did he just send all the hellhounds to their extinction?

Sure they looked terrifying, with their glowing red eyes and razor-sharp teeth, but they were just animals, coming from hell or not.

What had they done to deserve this brutal slaughter?

One of the hellhounds turned its attention to Damien, sensing his hesitation.

It charged at him, its jaws gaping wide. It didn't appear to give a flying fuck before it ripped his throat out, unlike him showing it sympathy just a second before.

Damien tripped on a tree branch, tumbling onto his backside. It dawned on him then that when he shifted into his wolf form, he was powerful because of Killian's blood. But now, in this human form, he was nothing more than a corporate man who used to love technology and skateboard shoes. Sure, he could throw a punch or two in the boxing ring at the gym, but he'd never be able to scuffle with a hellhound.

Now he understood why Killian had repeated himself so many times; telling him to meet with the mercenaries, give them directions, and immediately return to the Sanctuary. Damien didn't like it; turning away from a fight seemed weak. But now, sitting on his backside looking up at the gigantic dog lunging at him, if being weak was what would save his life, then so be it.

Suddenly, there was a blur of movement as Simba leaped out of nowhere, landing on the hellhound's back. The cat sank its claws into the hellhound's flesh, drawing blood. The hellhound yelped in pain and shook its body, trying to dislodge Simba.

But the little cat held on tight, snarling fiercely. As the hellhound thrashed around, it accidentally knocked one of the mercenaries, who stumbled and fell off the edge of a cliff.

The other mercenaries were too busy fighting to notice, but Damien saw everything. He rushed towards the fallen mercenary, hoping to grab his hand and pull him up before it was too late.

But he was too slow. The mercenary slipped through his fingers and fell to his death.

Damien felt sick to his stomach as he watched the body disappear into the misty abyss below.

The mercenaries were skilled, resourceful and ruthless.

However, they were no match for the sheer ferocity and numbers of the hell hounds.

"Damn it! Fall back!" one of the mercenaries shouted as another was dragged down by a pack of hounds, his screams quickly silenced by razor-sharp teeth.

"Shit, shit, shit," Damien cursed under his breath, firing off one last shot before turning to flee.

The lucky charm around his neck seemed to pulse with energy, allowing him to narrowly avoid the snapping jaws of a hell hound lunging at him.

Killian had said the hell hounds were merely big dogs from the Underworld. They knew they had an advantage when dealing with humans, so they wouldn't put up too much guard or be too cautious. But if they figured out those inside the house at the Sanctuary were wolf shifter, that would be a whole different ball game.

Damien had no choice; he wouldn't survive in his human form.

Taking a deep breath, he shifted into his furry wolf form and bared his teeth. In shock by witnessing the change, the hell hound stopped on its track.

"That should give me enough time to escape!" Damien thought to himself as he turned around, sprinting back toward the Sanctuary.

The hell hounds were now aware of the wolf shifters

within the Sanctuary. However, he would have to deal with that situation later; for now, the priority was on survival.

Out of the corner of his eye, he noticed Simba had hopped on his back for a ride.

He let the cat hang on, and promised himself he'd feed it and make sure it got anything it wanted for the rest of its natural life.

# SEVENTEEN

I vy trembled, her mind racing back to the gruesome sight of Damien sprinting home in his wolf form with his fur soaked in blood and poor Simba dangling from his back.

Both he and the cat weren't badly injured. But now the hell hounds knew exactly what lay inside the Sanctuary fence.

Ciaran trudged into the living room, his hands buried in his pockets.

Ivy had not known Ciaran for long, but she could already discern a pattern; whenever he was stuck with an intractable problem or a solution that didn't seem ideal, this was how he behaved.

"The mercenaries are all dead. Their tracking devices reported the head count. It's zero," Ciaran said.

Killian prowled the room. Viv quickly herded Simba and the other pets into the corner, calming them down. Nina examined Damien for any visible wounds.

Uncle Finn took inventory of their weapons at the rear of the house. Erin worked frantically on Killian's potion, allowing him to break the curse and shift into his wolf form to fight. Quinn and Fiona aided Erin in whatever she required for her work.

Erin's contribution was essential in this chess game - without her success, without Killian leading his pack beyond the fence, there seemed no hope left.

"Viv," Killian said, his voice taut with urgency, "reinforce the protective spell around the fence, please. Use your druidic spells to add to what Ivy had already gotten in place, but stay away from the fence itself."

"On it," Viv peeked outside, seeing nothing dangerous, she walked to the yard to do what Killian asked.

Ivy shuffled the cards again for fifth time. It was as if they were teasing or taunting her. The cards were blank.

"I can hit the hell hounds with my thunder bolts," Ciaran suggested."From this distance, it won't take much control and it won't cost me too much energy."

Killian shook his head. "No, Ciaran. It's too dangerous."

"Come on, Killian, we don't have many options left!" Ciaran protested, frustration creeping into his voice. "All I need you to do is to watch my back..."

"Just in case you fall?" Killian said, his voice firm but not unkind. "You can't control your power. Heck, you don't even know where it comes from. You can't recharge your energy quickly, or heal yourself from injuries like us. So if you're worn out or injured, what am I supposed to do with you?"

Ciaran clenched his fists, his jaw tight as he wrestled with the truth behind Killian's words.

Ivy saw the conflict in his eyes, the desire to help battling with the fear of exposing himself to danger greater than he could handle and became a liability to the group.

"Killian's right, Ciaran," Ivy said softly, placing a hand on his arm. "We need to find another way."

As they scrambled to come up with a plan, the howls of the hell hounds echoed in her ears like a haunting melody, a constant reminder of the threat looming ever closer, and their time is running out.

***

THE INCESSANT HOWLING of the hell hounds grew louder and more threatening, echoing through the dense forest surrounding the Sanctuary.

Killian's pack had been doing their best to keep the beasts at bay, employing every tactic they knew to slow down their advance. Wolves worked together in coordinated groups, weaving throughout the trees to create a labyrinth of obstacles for the ferocious hounds.

Ivy watched from behind the protective barrier she had cast around the Sanctuary, her heart heavy with the knowledge that their efforts were not enough.

She could see the fatigue in the wolves' movements, their fur matted with blood as they fought to protect their home.

"Damn it," she muttered under her breath, frustration mounting as another wolf fell lifeless to the ground.

A minor disturbance stirred within the house. Quinn frantically darted into the kitchen for a glass of water.

"What's going on?" Ivy asked.

"Erin collapsed. She had been slaving away without pause for twelve hours straight," Quinn explained breathlessly.

"I'll take care of it" Ivy replied calmly, before sprinting toward the barn where Erin had set up shop.

On the floor, Erin sat, leaning against a stack of hay, She was exhausted but still conscious. Ivy knelt down.

"Can I cast healing magic on you?"

Erin smiled. "No thanks. I'm fine. Really."

She helped Erin up and understood the reservations; her magic connected to the demon with side effects. In fact, only Killian and Ciaran would take her magic without reservation.

"Is there anything I can do to help hasten the process?"

"Do you know natural medicine?"

"No."

"That's what I need, unfortunately."

"Understood."

As if in answer to her desperation, the tarot cards Ivy had been using to try and gain insight into the situation began to vibrate with energy.

Her hands trembled as she drew a card, her heart sinking when she saw the image of betrayal and death depicted on its surface: The Death card. It wasn't the first time she had drawn this card, but it was different this time. As for what that the difference was, she didn't know.

"Killian," she called out as she ran towards the living room.

As if on cue, Killian met her there. Since their intimacy, their emotions were so tightly linked he could read her emotions before they spiked.

"What's the matter, Ivy?"

He looked her up and down, studying her closely.

"I drew the Death card. I've seen this before, but something seemed different this time... like it had to do with betrayal... like it was within your pack..."

"Impossible," he muttered.

"I know you don't believe me, Killian. I'm just telling you what I saw."

"The pack, those wolves out there are risking their lives to protect us because I can't go out myself.

"I understand that, Killian. But could you just double-check again? Please?"

"Fine, I'll speak to Uncle Finn about it."

Five minutes later, Killian re-entered the living room. "I can't find him." Not only did Ivy see concern etching on his face, she could feel his blood boiling with anxiety.

Ivy scrambled around the house, alerting everyone. They congregated in the living room. Viv crossed her arms over her chest.

"All right, this could be nothing. But I saw Finn leave with a couple of hulking wolves, headed to the far side of Sanctuary."

"When?" Ivy asked anxiously.

"Twenty minutes ago, maybe half an hour."

"That's more than enough time to get outside our protective fence," Killian snarled, and rushed toward the door.

"No, Killian, I'll go get him..." Damien stepped forward and shoved Killian aside.

He shifted into his wolf form before anyone had a chance to protest and ran outside.

***

As minutes ticked by like hours, Ivy paced anxiously, her heart pounding in her chest.

The howls outside only grew more intense, and she knew that the situation was becoming dire.

Finally, Damien emerged from the fog, stepping inside the fence, carrying Uncle Finn's lifeless body over his shoulders.

Ivy's breath caught in her throat at the sight, tears welling in her eyes.

Quinn, let out a gut-wrenching sob.

Since Killian's father passed away, and before Killian was of legal age, Finn was a crucial support in the household, in the pack. He held it all together until Killian was prepared.

Quinn's eyes shifted from their usual warm brown to a feral amber as she lost control of her emotions, succumbing to her tiger form.

Ivy knew that once she shifted, it would be nearly impossible to keep her inside the Sanctuary's fence.

"Mother, please," Killian pleaded, his voice cracking with emotion. "You can't go out there. I can't protect you right now. We need to stay together and find a way to stop these hell hounds."

"Killian is right," Ivy said firmly. "We need to focus on finding a solution, not taking any risks that would put our lives in danger. We can't help anyone if we're dead."

Viv cleared her throat. "He wasn't killed by the hounds." She gestured towards Finn's upper body.

"Could be other kind of animals. But these marks are lethal," Ciaran observed the deep claw marks on the jugular and around the throat.

"Not those wounds, Pretty Head, this." Viv pointed to her left temple.

Ivy stepped forward, examining the thumb-sized bruise on Finn's left temple. She didn't recognize this method of killing, but it certainly wasn't something that could have been caused by a hound or a werewolf.

"Where are the other bodies, Damien?" Ciaran asked.

"They were too decayed to be retrieved," he replied.

Their connection revealed to Ivy that Killian was distraught beyond measure, yet he remained composed and stood firmly beside his mother in case she became overwhelmed with emotion and shifted.

"So you're saying it was the mark that killed Finn, and not the gash in his body, Viv?" Ciaran asked.

"I'm no doctor, but I do remember seeing a ritual which used that same mark to kill someone when I was a child. I didn't even know it was still practiced nowadays."

"You think this is some kind of druidic magic then?" Ivy inquired.

"Oh no, this is much darker than that. The person who taught it must have come from very high powers. If you have enough money and can find someone who knows this kind of magic and is willing to teach it for payment...well then, yes, you can certainly learn it."

"But how do you know this is what killed Finn and the other wolves?"

"The druid that practiced this died a few years ago." She snorted. "Poisoned by his own drug! He tried to learn potion making from the dark witches, and it backfired. But, point is, when he performed this magic, he was offering to the god of the magic. He sacrificed people to gain more power. I was very little so, I hid behind a chest and I saw it all. These are things you can never forget."

"How did he do it?" Ivy asked.

"He chanted an incarnation, then placed his right thumb on the person left temple, he held up a bowl containing some kind of liquid on his left hand. Something sparked in the air and struck the water. Then there's light going through him, from the left hand, to the right hand and into the person's head. The person burnt into ash right in front of me."

"But Finn wasn't burned," Ciaran said.

Viv shook her head. "During the ritual, he set fire to two people. But when it came to the third one, it was like he ran out of steam. The sparks flickered from the water and onto the person's head. But the body didn't burn. That was how the clan found out about it and exiled him."

No one from my pack practices that kind of ritual," Killian declared. "This isn't something done by someone on the inside. It has all the markings of demons. They tricked us into releasing the hell hounds. Of course they'd want the hounds go all the way into the human world. But we keep their dogs contained in our territory. Obviously, it is in the demons' best interest to kill us and have their animals freed."

"If the demon we met in the Underworld wanted to kill us, he didn't have to go through all this trouble," Ivy said.

Killian paced back and forth, then nodded. "You're right. I wasn't thinking straight."

"Speak of the devil," Damien exclaimed, jabbing his finger at the front door of the house.

A short distance from the front of the Sanctuary, a group of hell hounds marched toward them.

One of the beasts broke away from the group and stepped closer to the fence line. It pulled back its snout and let out a loud howl before standing upright on two legs and transforming into a man.

"He's a wolf shifter turned hell hound." Killian said.

"The best hell hounds are wolf shifters, and that guy is a shifter and an alpha of that pack," Ivy muttered.

From a short distance outside the fence, he raised his voice and let the win carry the sound in.

"Is he speaking French? We have a French wolf shifter turned hell hound, are you kidding me?" Damien exclaimed.

Ciaran translated: "He demands to speak with the pack leader."

"He is not available, asshole," Nina bellowed in French.

Ciaran translated: "Either he comes out here and talks to me like a civilized person, or I will slaughter every one of you without mercy. Do not assume those flimsy fences are going to keep you safe."

# EIGHTEEN

Ivy watched Killian pacing the living room, his formerly calm composure lost when the alpha hell hound had challenged him right at his doorstep.

She readjusted her stance, so that if he decided to charge out the door, she would be able to tackle him and possibly knock him out before he got too far.

Hoping it wouldn't come to that, Ivy glanced at Ciaran, who had his hands in his pockets, standing still at the back of the room and observing. He gave her a curt nod, suggesting they were on the same page.

Ciaran read combat situations like the palm of his hand - he knew how the situation would escalate and what they should do to gain an advantage or hold their ground. He was also aware of their weak points, and Killian's temperament was one of them.

Killian growled, "we know these hell hounds behave like wolves in my pack. If we kill their leader, the rest will succumb. That's our best shot at stopping this impending attack."

Ciaran nodded, raking a hand through his raven dark hair. "You're right, Killian. But what if the hound leader challenged you because he knew you couldn't shift right now? If he isn't afraid of the fence as he claimed, wouldn't he be in here right now? Why would he need to lure you out?"

"The hounds saw Damien shift," Killian responded. "If they can make any assumptions on that, then they should assume all of us can shift."

"Not if someone tells him you're the only one in your pack who can't shift," Fiona said.

"Traitors don't belong to my pack—they get killed like Adam!" Killian snarled.

Ivy stepped between Fiona and Killian. "All right, that doesn't help. The immediate problem we need to solve is that the alpha out there is challenging Killian and he's waiting for a response. We don't know how credible his threat is or his capacity..."

"He has shit loads of hell dogs," Viv said, patting the crow that had landed on her arm when she reached her hand out the window. "My little lookout just flew over the hell hound area."

As Viv glanced around the room, her eyes changed from raven black to her usual soft grey. She continued.

"They have plenty of hounds standing near their leader at our fence. But in the hills, they must have close to a hundred saliva-dripping red-eyed dogs waiting."

"Then we need more people," Ivy suggested, her jaw tightening. "But money won't buy us the help we require."

"You're right," Ciaran sighed, rubbing his temples.

"The last time we hired mercenaries for protection, they all ended up dead. Ordinary humans, no matter how capable, can't fight against hell hounds."

"Let's focus on what we can handle," Ivy said, her gaze fixing on Killian's face. "We need to find a way to break the curse and send these hell hounds back to where they belong."

Erin rose from the chair, tucked away in the corner of the room. "I am almost finished mixing the potion that will break the curse." She nodded toward Killian. "And you aren't going anywhere outside that fence without the potion."

Quinn paced restlessly about the room as Fiona tapped her fingers against the table, her fiery red hair framing her visage as she leaned forward.

"We could use shifters' help," Quinn proposed to Killian. "Between lynx and tiger shifters, we can match the numbers of hell-hounds."

Fiona nodded in agreement. "That should do it — much better than sitting here feeling helpless."

"You can't exactly phone the tiger and lynx shifters for help," Killian said. "They don't have the ability to communicate telepathically, last time I checked. You have talked to them directly. If going outside the fence to talk to them directly isn't an option for me right now, it's not for you two either."

Ciaran shook his head. "Even if you could get extra help from other shifters, it would still be a bloodbath. And there's still no guarantee that we won't become casualties too. It's not a fair fight, because those things coming from hell are already dead. We can't kill them twice."

Nina wrinkled her nose. "If we can't fight them directly, can we just hurl them back to the Underworld like they're sheep?"

Ciaran chuckled. "That's a good idea, Nina. But they aren't sheep, and we need an incredibly strong reason for them to willingly go back to their hell hole. Sure I can open up a portal, just like leading a horse to water, but someone will have to make them actually drink."

Killian frowned. "You can crack open a portal close to the fence?"

Ciaran shrugged. "With great effort on my part, yes. I'm not sure how close to the fence. But it will have to be outside the fence, not inside, or I'll blow our own assess off. And also, I'll be incapacitated after I've done that."

Killian nodded. "If we can open the gateway to the Underworld, I can ask Father to take the hounds there. But we still need a reason for them to follow my Father."

"How about a fake pardon from the gods," Ivy said. "These hounds were from the hell jail. That must have committed a sin or two to be in there. So, if we can tell them they are forgiven by the gods, but they have to go back and accept the pardon, would that work?"

"That's brilliant," Ciaran grinned. "Do you know what a pardon should look like?"

Nina chipped in. "This guy was speaking ancient French - how old do you reckon he is?"

Killian stated: "Judging by the look of the jail before we broke them out, that venue hasn't been touched for at least hundreds of years."

"Right, so, he's very old and probably hasn't seen this." Nina pulled out her cell phone and quickly typed with her thumbs.

In a short moment, she showed everyone a glowing golden background with archaic font text printed on it.

"This is an app, a prototype I've been developing. Do you think this would work?"

Damien squinted. "If I'm a hundred of years old, and I have never seen technology before - hell yeah, I believe this has come from heaven! Of course, if the wording is right, because I haven't got the slightest idea."

"The wording is perfect," Ciaran said.

"All right, I'll call my father, then," Killian said, "I'll take the phone out to the alpha."

Ivy shook her head. "No, you're not going outside, Killian. You stay here, right next to Erin, and as soon as she finishes that potion, you can take it and go where you please."

"Do you speak French, Ivy?" Nina asked.

"No," replied Ivy.

"I didn't think so," Nina said before raising her index finger to stop them from speaking. "I'll take the phone out to the hound because I know how to work the app and I speak French; plus Damien will be with me just in case something goes wrong. And Ivy has to stay with Ciaran because once he opens the gateway he'll be drained of energy and you have to use your healing magic to fix him. Any objections?"

She continued on without waiting for a response. "Good, I didn't think so because it's a brilliant plan. You can call your father now, Killian."

. . .

***

Operating in the cramped room wasn't ideal, but Ciaran had wanted to be alone. He had preferred to be out in the open air, but the pesky hound was blocking his path in the front yard.

He knew they could do it.

Admittedly he hadn't done this before, but he thought it best not to tell his team. They needed a confidence boost and revealing the truth now wouldn't help them.

Harnessing electricity from the sky and hurling thunderbolts at a distance was easy for him as it only relied on natural energy—he didn't have to control either the actions or consequences.

All he had to do previously was throw; if he missed, it didn't make a difference.

But now, not only did he need to open a portal in the veil, but it had to be right at their doorstep. Missing the mark simply wasn't an option.

Hearing the sound from behind him, he turned and saw ivy, leaning against the door frame.

"I need to do this alone, Ivy."

"But you can't heal yourself. I won't interfere, I promise." She closed the door behind her.

There was no point in arguing. They didn't have the time. So, he got on with the work.

He closed his eyes, concentrating on drawing energy

from the air around him as his hands crackled with electricity.

"Come on, Ciaran," he whispered to himself, clenching his fists as the first tendrils of lightning began to form. "You can do this."

With a deep breath, he thrust his hands forward, unleashing a powerful bolt of lightning towards the ground.

The thunderbolt struck with a resounding crash, and a small fissure opened in the earth – the beginnings of a portal.

Ciaran's knees buckled under the strain, sweat beading on his forehead, blood dropped down from his nose to the carpet as he fought to maintain control over the raw power coursing through him.

He knew he had to make the portal larger, but each attempt drained more of his strength.

"Almost there," he gasped, gritting his teeth as he sent another bolt of lightning crashing into the fissure.

"You hit the right spot, Ciaran. The gate is opening," Ivy said.

"I know ..."

The edges of the portal widened, its dark maw yawning like the entrance to the underworld itself.

"Is that enough?" Ivy asked.

"No... I need a bit more."

He could feel his body swaying and he was on the verge of collapsing. Ivy's steady hand wrapped around his shoulders.

His vision began to darken and he felt like he was drowning. But he needed one more push.

He concentrated, summoning all of the strength he had left to blast one final time.

Then everything went black.

"ALL RIGHT, LET'S GO," Nina said to Damien.

Outside the fence, they gazed in awe at the gateway Ciaran had opened. It was like a haven gate to them. If her app held up and her theory proved true that these hounds had never encountered technology before, then their chances of success were encouragingly high.

As they headed out of the fence toward the portal, Damien tugged on her elbow.

"If there is a fight, you must stay close behind me, okay?"

"Got it!"

On cue, Ayden ambled in and stood just inside the gate. Nina and Damien steadily marched toward the gate from the right, and a hulking figure came over from the left.

The leader of the hound revealed himself as a tall man with broad shoulders and an athletic build. He was handsome, but he had an aura of danger radiating off him like heat. His eyes were a deep abyss, and his lips thinned into a sinister smirk.

"What is this ostentatious display?" I demanded of the alpha of your pack. "Is he too cowardly to accept the challenge?"

Nina smiled. "Greeting!"

"Oh milady!" The hound's tone instantly calmed

down when he saw Nina in the halo of light from the portal.

She knew she had that effect on men; they generally liked her face. She heard a low growl of jealousy in Damien's throat, so she made a mental note to address that with him later.

"I'm not a shapeshifter, I'm sure you can tell," she pointed at Damien. "The Alpha of the pack sent his deputy to escort me; if he had accepted your challenge before showing this, then this conversation wouldn't be happening. He thinks it would be unfair to you."

"How so?"

Nina gestured toward Ayden inside the portal. "I represent the House of Gods in the human realm; the gods have pardoned you for the sin you committed and now believe that you have redeemed yourself. That is, if no further sins are committed."

The hound stepped back slightly.

She had hit him with an uncomfortable truth and she knew it.

She continued. "You know you're not allowed to interact with creatures from other realms without proper cause. That's a grave sin. But our Alpha understands that you ran through the gateway by accident and killed those men in self-defense. So if you return whence you came, knowing you have been pardoned, our Alpha is willing to forgive the deaths and will not report your trespass into the human realm or the killings to your gods."

"What's in it for him then?"

"A favor. Next time, when he needs a favor from the Underworld, he will call for you."

The hound contemplated. "That's fair. Show me the god's seal of pardon."

Nina presented him with the glowing cell phone in her hand.

He stepped forward to reach it, but she raised a hand to prevent him from coming any closer.

"This is my carrier. You cannot have it. I am the messenger. If you don't believe me, then you can confirm with your gods. If it turns out that the information is not true, then you can always return here for a new challenge.

The hound shifter narrowed its eyes, weighing the situation, torn between suspicion and the allure of salvation.

Nina held her breath.

"Fine," the shifter growled. "I accept."

With that, the hellhounds began to file through the portal, their massive forms disappearing into the swirling darkness beyond.

Nina watched them go, counting each one, hoping against hope that they would all return to the depths from which they had come.

"Wait!" A shrill cry rang out, making Nina's heart leap into her throat.

A twisted creature emerged from the shadows, its bony form wrapped in tattered rags. Its hollow eyes bore into Ivy with a chilling intensity.

"They lie!"

A wave of panic washed over Nina, her mind racing to find a solution.

She forced herself to smile at the hound shifter. "This is your only chance at redemption; don't squander it. Would you listen to me, a representative of the House of Gods, or listen to that thing?" She pointed at the creature.

The man looked at his hounds to calm them. But the damage had been done. The remaining hounds hesitated, glancing between their leader and the skeletal figure before them.

Even as half of the pack vanished into the portal, the others began to growl and snarl.

"Run!" Damien yelled. "Get back inside!"

Nina's heart was pounding as they sprinted away from the gateway, with the howls of their pursuers growing louder every second. She felt her lungs burning, but she kept on pushing herself, knowing that safety awaited them in the Sanctuary.

"Keep going! We can make it!" Nina encouraged him.

"Almost there," she panted, her muscles aching painfully as they reached the Sanctuary's entrance. "Just a little further..."

With one final burst of speed, Damien and Nina raced past the fence line into the sanctuary.

The sound of howling and snarling echoed from behind them. Nina glanced over her shoulder. The hell hounds stayed clear of the fence surrounding the Sanctuary; Ivy's protective spells had done their job .

For now.

# NINETEEN

Killian stood at the window, his chest tight with the weight of responsibility.

He watched as Nina, and Damien stumbled through the fence their clothes torn and faces smeared with soot.

Their frantic panting was the only sound he could register, a sharp reminder of the hell hounds that had chased them across the field right in front of his home.

"Damn it," Killian muttered under his breath.

As the alpha, it was his duty to protect his people, but the curse had left him powerless and vulnerable. The guilt gnawed at him like a persistent itch he couldn't scratch.

And Ivy... the realization that he loved her sent a surge of warmth through his veins, followed by an icy fear.

She was more than just a member of his pack now; she was everything.

He spun around and saw Ivy walking up to him. "How's Ciaran?"

She shook her head. "He just woke up. He's still in very bad shape. I don't understand it. When the demon attacked him, he looked way worse off. But as soon as I used healing magic on him, he was back up, running around like nothing happened. Now, there isn't a single bruise on him. How can he be so sick?"

"Those powers he used have caused a lot of damage internally, Ivy. It's like spending money you don't have. He hasn't fully earned that power yet, so when he uses it, this is what happens."

Killian walked with Ivy towards Ciaran's room.

Ciaran was getting off the bed as they entered. Ivy quickly rushed over to him.

"Hey, what are you doing?"

"I'm all right, Ivy. Did the portal work?"

Nina barged her way into the room. "Yes, it worked. We managed to get rid of half of the hounds. It's a pity that not all of them returned to hell. But now we've got a smaller number, and Mom and Quinn went out to recruit more shifters, so we're in much better shape than before."

Damien tried to squeeze his way in but the room was already full, so he stayed at the door.

"We still have half of the hellhounds to deal with. Why don't we gather the pack and attack them before they can regroup and come up with a new strategy?"

A chorus of howls resounded into the house.

"It appears they already have a fresh plan," Killian uttered.

A primal roar built up inside of him, urging him to tear down the fences that protected them from the hell hounds and face the enemy head-on. He couldn't stand being trapped, waiting for death to find them.

He took a step toward the door.

Ciaran's voice stopped Killian dead in his tracks.

"Where do you think you're going?" Ciaran asked, incredulous.

Killian replied with a low and controlled tone, "Out there, to fight those bastards."

Ciaran scoffed, "Okay, if you have a burning desire to be slaughtered, that's fine by me. But I don't want to become dog food. So why don't you let me call my people? They'll pick me up in a chopper and then when I'm out of here safe and sound, you can go out and get yourself killed. How does that sound?"

"Better to die an alpha than cower behind these walls," Killian snapped.

Ciaran shrugged and then winced from the pain he was in. "There are smart and worthy ways to die. And there are stupid ways to die. I refuse to go the stupid way. And I don't think you care for that either, Killian.

"It doesn't matter, Ciaran. I have a curse upon me and no matter how hard I try, I can't seem to break it..."

"Killian!" Erin's desperate plea reverberated through the hallway as she shoved aside those in her way. Bursting into the room, a small vial clutched in her hand, she exclaimed," I've done it! I've completed the potion using the sample you brought back from the underworld. This will break the curse-you'll be able to shift into your wolf form whenever and as many times as you want..."

"Are you sure?" Killian asked, his gaze intent.

"Positive," Erin responded, presenting him with the vial.

Without a second thought, Killian snatched up the vial, his hands shaking lightly.

He could feel the expectation inside of him amplify as he uncorked it and lifted it to his lips.

As the potion ran down his throat, he felt an influx of power rush through his body, invigorating him.

It was as if every cell in his being had come alive.

"By the gods," Killian whispered, sensing the curse ease its grasp on him.

A myriad of feelings stormed through him – relief, appreciation, and new resolution.

He glanced at Ivy, his love for her shining from his eyes.

"Thank you, Erin," he said quietly,"You've given me an opportunity to fight for my people."

As Killian's words lingered in the air, the room became silent.

Ivy, Damien, and Nina exchanged glances, each understanding the importance of this moment and what this newfound freedom meant for Killian.

An evident sense of hope began to fill the room, mixing with the remaining tension.

"Now I can contact the so-called alpha hellhound shifter!" Killian spun around to head into the living room.

Erin followed behind him.

"What do you mean by speaking to him, Killian?"

"The hellhound out there is challenging me. I'm

going to have a civilized discussion with him. And if we can't sort out our differences peacefully, then so be it, I'll take his challenge – I'll shift and we will fight. That's how I always run the pack; I thought you knew that, Erin?"

"Be careful, Killian," Ivy asked, her voice wavering slightly. "Can I come with you?"

Erin shook her head firmly. "Killian, you need to shift before going outside the fence. The hounds are unpredictable – they could ambush you!"

"Erin," Killian said calmly but firmly, "I want to negotiate with their leader first. If I shift, I won't be able to speak to them. And besides, I don't condone violence if it can be avoided."

"Those hell hounds aren't to be trusted!" Erin argued, her concern evident. "You're putting yourself in danger by trying to reason with them."

"I appreciate your concern, Erin, but I must do what I believe is best for our people. My decision is final."

Erin templed before finally giving in, nodding reluctantly.

As Killian reached the main entrance of the house, Viv shouted from the rear door. She had just entered from the back garden.

"Killian! Erin is your traitor!"

Viv's statement made everyone freeze in their tracks.

Gasps filled the room.

Killian stood frozen, unable to process what he'd just heard. Anger and disbelief warred inside him as he stared at Erin, the woman he'd once loved.

"Viv, what did you just say?" Killian meant to ask, but his words came out in a menacing growl.

Vivian held a raven in her hands, as she raised its feet for the ritual. "It's a druidic custom to mourn the dead. I don't know much of these rituals, but this one--I do it often. I ask them questions, I comfort them, and I listen to their last words. When I tried praying to my deceased parent, you'll never guess what I saw--you fucking dark witch..." Vivian screamed and lunged at Erin.

Nina rushed over and restrained Viv as her sobs shook her body.

"I know you won't believe me. But that bird shared its final vision with me, like its dying words, so that I can pray for it. It saw Erin killing Finn at the fence. It saw her dropping her blood into your potion, Killian. It's just the words of a dead bird. My words against hers. I know you won't beleive me...."

"I believe you, Viv," Ciaran said firmly.

"Enough!" Erin snarled, rage dripping from her words as she lunged toward Vivian. But Killian was quicker, stepping in front of her and blocking her path.

"Tell me the truth, Erin," he demanded. "We were once lovers. Even if we didn't work out, why would you destroy the good moments we had? I cherished our love."

"Cherished?" Erin scoffed sarcastically, her eyes narrowing. "You never took my love seriously, Killian. You dismissed it like it meant nothing."

"Is that why you did this? Why you betrayed us all?"

"This pack robbed me of my happiness. You told me we weren't a good fit. The alpha position means everything to you and you needed the best mate for the pack. I understood. I believed you. But it was a total lie. You declared your love for this...bitch - a total misfit. She's not even a shifter. And guess what? You're going to change the rules for her - you're going to change the pack's rules to fit her in. How do you think it made me feel?"

"You can do anything to me to get your revenge. Why did you kill Finn?"

"He was in the wrong place at the wrong time. He saw me go out for my ritual practice. Yeah, I practice dark magic. I can break a curse as easily as I conjure it, Killian. I am the best asset for your pack, not her."

"I can forgive anything you did to me; for old times' sake. But I cannot forgive you for killing Finn."

She chuckled and smiled through tears. "I mixed my blood with the potion you took! But I did it because I still love you, Killian. The potion is pure; I indeed completed it; you can shift now, it has broken the curse for you. But if you shift, our souls will be bound--in the eyes of the gods, we are soulmates, in life and death."

"Erin, you're gravely mistaken," Killian said. "Even if I die because of this twisted plan of yours, I will never return to you. If I have to go to hell because I don't want to be with you, then I choose hell over you."

His words hung heavy in the air and the tension in the room was palpable.

Erin's face contorted with anguish and fury as she processed what he had just told her.

"Then you've made your choice," Erin hissed, anger evident in her voice.

She stepped back, her body trembling as her ex-lover effectively severed any remaining ties between them.

"Erin, wait—" Killian started, but it was too late.

Before anyone could respond, Erin threw her head back, letting out a howl that reverberated through the living room.

Her body shifted and contorted as bones cracked and reshaped, transforming her into her wolf form.

With one last sorrowful glance toward Killian, she bolted past the stunned onlookers and sprinted for the door.

"Erin, no!" Killian shouted, realizing her intentions. He raced after her, desperate to stop her from facing the hell hounds alone.

But when he reached the threshold, the gruesome scene unfolding before him froze him in his tracks.

In mere moments, the hell hound leader had seized Erin's wolf form in its powerful jaws, her anguished cries ringing through the night air.

Blood splattered the ground as the enormous beast tore into her, shaking her body violently before flinging it aside like a rag doll.

The pack of hounds snarled and snapped, their thirst for bloodshed insatiable as they descended upon Erin's lifeless form.

"Erin!" Killian screamed, his voice hoarse with grief and rage. He dropped to his knees, tears streaming down his cheeks as he watched the woman who had once loved him meet her violent end.

# TWENTY

I vy stood in front of Killian, eyes burning with a searing rage and a fear that seemed to shake her whole being.

The fragrant scent of rain and earth filled the air around them while dark clouds roared angrily above, mirroring the conflicting emotions brewing deep inside her chest.

She knew what he had to do. She understood, yet her selfish love for him didn't want him to go through with it

The ground shook beneath them, and Ivy's heart raced in her chest as the Sanctuary's fence line groaned under the relentless force of the hell hounds.

The once-peaceful haven for animals and wildlife was now a battleground as the beasts clawed their way through Ivy's protective spells.

"How long would it take your helicopter to get here, Ciaran?" Killian asked.

"You're fucking kidding me, right?"

"I'm dead serious. Everyone has to leave. The hounds

are here because of me, and I'll fight them off. As for my pack – anyone who wants to stay with me can, and those who don't can run off to another territory. I won't hold that against them."

The hounds outside pounded at the fence, which was weakening by the second.

"If anyone here needs me to call a chopper, raise your hands." Ciaran asked.

No one responded.

"So you've got your answer, Killian. Are you going to take the lead of your pack now? Or do you need me to?" Ciaran said.

"Killian!" Ivy shouted, her voice barely audible over the cacophony of snarls, growls, and terrified animal cries. "They're breaking through!"

"Everyone, get ready!" Killian commanded. "Ivy, Ciaran, Damien – stay close! Nina, Viv, keep to the back!"

As if responding to Killian's words, the fence finally gave way, and the monstrous hell hounds poured into the Sanctuary.

Their dark fur bristled with malice, and their red eyes glowed like embers in the night.

Ivy watched in horror as they tore apart the peaceful surroundings, uprooting trees and crushing delicate plants under their massive paws.

The air became thick with the scent of blood and fear.

"Listen up!" Killian yelled, his voice cutting through the chaos. "These hell hounds are using pack combat techniques – they're encircling us, pushing us back toward the house. They'll try to separate us into smaller groups to pick us off one by one. We have to stay together if we want to survive this!"

"Got it, Killian," Ciaran replied, his hands already gripping the guns at his sides.

"Understood," Damien said, drawing his hunting knife and dagger with a determined expression.

From the corner of her eye, Ivy saw Nina clutching a long fishing spear, while Vivian held a handful of hound deterrent herbs, ready to throw them at any approaching beast. She hoped it would be enough to keep them safe.

"Stay close, everyone," Killian repeated. "We'll make our stand together."

Ivy nodded, swallowing the lump in her throat. As much as she feared losing Killian to these monstrous creatures, she knew they had no choice but to fight – not just for themselves, but for everything they held dear.

And as she gripped her own small hunting knives, Ivy vowed that she would do whatever it took to protect those she loved.

***

THE CLASH of metal against monstrous flesh and the deafening snarls of the hell hounds filled the air as Ivy, Killian, and the others fought desperately to hold their ground.

Ciaran's guns roared, bullets tearing through the hounds' ethereal hides, though they seemed to barely slow them down.

Killian's daggers whirled like silver wind, slicing deep but never quite finding a fatal blow.

Damien's knife and dagger danced in his hands, drawing blood and eliciting cries of pain from the beasts.

"Keep them back!" Killian bellowed, sweat beading on his brow as his eyes darted between the encroaching creatures. "Don't let them break our formation!"

Nina, her face pale but determined, brandished her fishing spear with trembling hands. With each lunge of a hell hound, she stabbed forward, forcing them to retreat.

Vivian, meanwhile, hurled handfuls of herbs at the snarling beasts, which recoiled in disgust as the plants turned to writhing worms upon contact.

"Stay away, you monsters!" Vivian screamed, her voice shrill with fear.

Ivy fought alongside them, her hunting knives flashing as she cut down one hound after another, frustration mounting as they continued to rise again.

Gritting her teeth, she tried to clear enough space so that she could use her magic without harming the others.

"Dammit," she muttered, parrying a snapping jaw before driving her knife into the hound's side. It collapsed, only to rise once more, its wounds healing before her very eyes.

"Focus, Ivy!" Killian shouted, sensing her growing despair. "We can do this!"

With a deep breath, Ivy allowed her senses to expand, reaching out to the hounds' souls.

She felt their vicious, dark energy pulsing around her, and she focused her will, yanking at the nearest soul.

The hound howled in agony as its essence was ripped away, leaving behind a lifeless husk.

"Come on, come on," Ivy whispered under her breath, repeating the process with another hound. It took all her concentration to maintain control, but each time she succeeded, another hellish creature fell.

"Keep it up, Ivy!" Damien called out, his face streaked with blood from a slash across his cheek. "We're making progress!"

But as Ivy's gaze shifted toward the hound alpha, her heart clenched.

Killian and the alpha beast were locked in a fierce duel, their weapons clashing violently.

She hesitated, knowing that she couldn't risk accidentally tearing Killian's soul away in an attempt to reach the hound leader.

"Stay alive, Killian," she murmured, praying for his safety as she continued to rip the souls from the lesser hounds.

And with each soul torn away, the hope of victory grew, even as the battle raged on around them.

***

"WATCH OUT!" Ciaran yelled as he threw a grenade, striking down several incoming hounds. The blast shook the ground and illuminated the chaos in blinding white light.

"Nice blast!" Killian shouted, slicing through another hound with his daggers.

Blood sprayed into the air as the creature crumpled to the ground, temporarily incapacitated.

"Keep moving!" Damien called out, panting heavily. He had sustained a deep gash on his arm, but fought on bravely, managing to hold off a pair of hounds with his hunting knife and dagger.

As Ciaran turned to check on the others, an opportunistic hound lunged at him from behind.

Its teeth bared and eyes gleaming with bloodlust, it aimed for his throat.

Ivy's heart raced as she reached for the creature's soul, focusing her energy and tearing its soul away.

"Thank you," Ciaran gasped, stumbling back from the lifeless body of the hound.

His eyes locked onto Ivy's, and she could see the concern etched across his face.

"We'll get through this, Ivy. Help is coming. Just don't engage with that underworld practice anymore. Stick with your knives," Ciaran said.

"Understood," Ivy nodded, though her mind raced with doubt.

Her ability to reap souls might be their only chance at survival, but the cost weighed heavy on her conscience.

"Stay together!" Killian ordered, wincing from a fresh wound on his side. The hounds were relentless, and every time one fell, two more seemed to materialize in its place.

"Damn it," Ciaran cursed, his exhaustion evident. "There's too many of them." Despite his fatigue, he continued to fire his guns, taking down hounds left and right.

"Killian!" Ivy cried, seeing him struggle against the sheer number of hounds.

She knew he was holding back, trying to protect her as well as fight off the beasts.

It broke her heart to see him in pain, but she couldn't risk using her magic on the hounds surrounding him.

"Stay focused!" Damien shouted, his voice strained with effort. A hound had managed to bite into his leg, but he held it at bay with the last of his strength.

***

"Viv, Nina, watch out!" Ivy cried, her heart pounding as she saw a group of hounds charging towards them. The two women were cornered against the house, their backs to the wall. Nina held her fishing spear defensively while Vivian clutched a bunch of hound-deterrent herbs in her hands. Despite the chaos, the women's faces showed determination and fearlessness.

"Stay back!" Vivian shouted, brandishing the herbs at the advancing hounds as if they were a weapon. "These will turn you into worms!"

"Viv, do you really think that'll work?" Nina asked skeptically, but she didn't miss a beat with her spear, jabbing it at any hound that came close.

"Can't hurt to try," Viv replied grimly.

"Damn it," Ivy muttered, desperately trying to find

an opening to help them without risking yanking out the souls of her friends on accident.

But every time she tried, another hound lunged at her, forcing her to defend herself with her own hunting knives.

Out of nowhere, a roar echoed through the sanctuary, silencing the cacophony of snarls and growls.

A roaring stampede of tigers surged from the shadows of the trees. The leader, Quinn, an enormous tigress with deep-golden fur and shimmering green eyes, bounded ahead. At her side was Fiona, a fierce lynx sporting stripes that shone like moonlight on midnight waters. Behind them marched an army of tiger and lynx shifters, their pelts ranging from pale cream to dark ebony as they readied for battle.

"About time you showed up!" Ciaran called out, relief evident in his voice.

"Couldn't let you have all the fun," Quinn responded with a smirk, slicing through a hellhound with her massive claws.

"Everyone, keep fighting!" Fiona urged, her voice fierce and commanding. She tore into the hounds with savage ferocity, ripping through them like they were mere shadows.

For a moment, it felt like they had the upper hand.

The tide turned as the tigers leapt from the trees, catching the hounds off guard. The roars set everyone's nerves on edge as they scattered in different directions. The forest became chaotic with animals running and screaming.

Ivy could see Killian, Ciaran, and Damien using this opportunity to regroup and launch a counterattack.

"Come on, we can do this!" Ivy yelled.

She sliced through a hound as it lunged at her, its snarl turning into a yelp of pain.

"Keep pushing!" Killian shouted, his daggers flashing in the sunlight as he fended off more hounds.

But even as they fought back, Ivy knew they were still outnumbered.

The hounds seemed endless, their numbers only growing stronger despite the tigers' best efforts.

"Stay strong," she whispered to herself, steeling her resolve as she prepared for the next wave of hellhounds. "We've come too far to give up now."

***

THE ALPHA SHIFTER hound - a massive beast with glowing red eyes and barbs protruding from its spine, reared back and unleashed an ear-splitting roar that shook the ground beneath them.

The sound was like metal scraping against metal, sending shivers down Ivy's spine.

As she watched the monstrous hound, it seemed to draw in power from the chaos and violence around it, becoming even stronger and more fearsome.

"Oh no, oh shit." Killian wouldn't shift. He fought in his human form. He took Erin's threat seriously, the if he shifted, his soul would be bound to Erin's forever.

"Killian, watch out!" she screamed, her voice cracking with fear as she saw the hound leader lunge at him, its vicious jaws open wide and aimed straight for his throat.

Killian tried to dodge, but the sheer force and speed of the attack caught him off-guard.

Ivy's heart pounded with terror.

In a moment of desperation, Ivy knew what she must do. She called upon Selene.

"Selene, please," she pleaded, tears spilling down her cheeks. "Help us."

"Do you accept our agreement, Ivy? Do you swear on your soul? All you have to do is say the word.

"Yes. Goddess Selene, I accept all we have discussed."

A sudden burst of light filled the sanctuary, blinding everyone momentarily.

When Ivy opened her eyes, she saw that the hounds had been captured in a flash, their monstrous forms held in place by an invisible force.

With another flicker of light, the hounds were gone, removed from the human realm and leaving behind a devastating battlefield.

Killian gasped, clutching his throat where the hound's fangs had almost connected.

He stared at Ivy, a mixture of relief and confusion on his face.

"Thank Selene," she whispered, tears still streaming down her cheeks as she approached him.

Across the field, Ciaran watched her with a mixture of gratitude and concern, shaking his head ever so slightly.

She knew what that gesture meant. Ciaran knew she had called Selene. More importantly, he understood why she did.

Ivy approached Killian.

"Are you all right?" she asked, touching his arm gently.

"Yes, and you?" He checked her up and down. The Killian locked eyes with her. "You forgot one thing, Ivy."

"What?"

"We're connected. Our hearts and our souls. I can feel you and your fear. I know you called the goddess. If you don't want to tell me the detail of your agreement with her now, I will wait. But I won't give up and pretend it didn't happen."

She nodded. "I just need some time."

"Take all the time you need." He kissed her forehead.

And as they stood there amidst the carnage, surrounded by the remnants of the fierce battle, Ivy knew that whatever consequences awaited her for calling upon Selene, she would face them head-on. After all, some things were worth fighting for – and love, she realized, was the strongest force of all.

CHAPTER

# TWENTY-ONE

The moon cast an eerie glow upon the Sanctuary, its once-pristine grounds now marred by the aftermath of the hell hound attack. Killian stared out his bedroom window, taking in the scene below—the scorched earth and the fallen trees that bore testament to their fierce battle.

The air still held a faint tang of sulfur and burnt wood.

He shuddered at the memory of the snarling beasts they had fought off only hours ago.

"Killian," Ivy called softly, snapping him back to the present.

In the dim light filtering through the curtains, her eyes shone with concern. She was tending to his wounds, her skilled hands working deftly as she applied a healing salve to the gashes on his arm.

Her touch was gentle, yet firm, and the soothing sensation of her magic made him feel both vulnerable and grateful under her care.

225

"Thank you," he murmured, his gaze fixed on the way her fingers moved over his skin.

As she worked, a cascade of her raven hair tumbled forward, framing her face like an ebony curtain. He reached up to caress her locks, brushing them behind her ear.

As she finished applying the salve, her movements slowed significantly, as if relishing every inch of his skin. The languid touch of her fingers exploring every dip in his muscles made his body thrum with anticipation.

The unhurried pace spoke volumes; she was in control and wanted to take charge - and he willingly surrendered to her every whim.

All the while, the heady aroma of lavender emanated from the salve, heightening the sensory experience for both of them.

Her movements were slower, more deliberate, and he caught a hint of something else in her eyes—a smoldering intensity that sent a thrill down his spine.

"Do you trust me?," Ivy whispered, her voice sultry and confident as she guided Killian back onto the bed.

"Always."

He hesitated briefly but then relaxed under her touch, allowing her to take control.

She straddled him, a wicked gleam in her eyes that sent shivers down his spine.

The air around them seemed to thrum with energy as Ivy lifted her hands, her fingers glowing with a soft white light. Killian watched, mesmerized, as she traced intricate patterns in the air above him. He could feel the power of her magic coursing through him, heightening his senses and intensifying his desire for her.

Ivy's warm breath tickled his ear as she whispered, "Trust me." A shiver ran through him, and before he could answer, they were lifted off the ground. Their bodies were buoyed by a cushion of magic air, and it felt like their souls were soaring. They were floating together in perfect harmony. The sensation was so thrilling that he wanted to stay there forever.

As they floated, she straddle him again. Their body fit perfectly.

and she pushed.

Their movements intertwined in perfect synchronization, each caress and touch setting off a blaze of desire within him that threatened to engulf them both. As the fire raged through their souls, Killian savored every stroke of Ivy's fingertips along his spine, the warmth of her lips searing through his flesh, and the thunderous beat of their hearts resonating in unison.

When she drove him to the highest peak, he tightly held her hands.

"No, Ivy. I want us to be united, in heart, body and soul."

He smoothly turned her over so that she could rest on an airy pillow of magic.

His tongue explored each inch of her body with meticulousness, savoring her dips and curves.

She was ready for him: utterly aroused and eager to give. He felt the warmth of her wetness enveloping him like a lullaby.

He drove Ivy to her climax.

Again.

And Again

Until her body tremble beneath him. As she cried out his name, her voice a beautiful, desperate plea. The sight of her in the throes of passion sent Killian over the edge as well, and he joined her in blissful ecstasy.

Only when their breathing had returned to normal and the lingering tremors of pleasure had subsided did Killian dare to ask again.

"Ivy, please," he urged softly, his fingers tracing the curve of her cheek. "Tell me what's on your mind."

"Later," she whispered, pressing a tender kiss to his lips. "When the time is right."

Though his curiosity burned within him, Killian knew better than to press her further. For now, he would simply bask in the warmth of her embrace, cherishing every second they had together before reality inevitably came crashing back down around them.

When their passion finally abated, Killian held Ivy close, enjoying the feel of her body as she lay spent in his arms. They drifted off to sleep, wrapped in each other's warmth and love.

THE COLD MORNING light filtered through the bedroom window, casting long shadows across the floor. Killian awoke with a start, his heart pounding as he realized Ivy was no longer in his arms.

The warmth of her body had vanished, replaced by a chilling sense of emptiness that threatened to swallow him whole.

His wolf senses strained to find any trace of her, but the room was eerily quiet, devoid of Ivy's comforting presence.

That's when he saw it – a small piece of parchment folded neatly on the pillow beside him.

Killian unfolded the note and began to read:

*KILLIAN,*

*I'm sorry I didn't tell you this sooner. I've made a deal with Selene to save us all.*

*But it comes at a cost: I've sold my soul.*

*In return, you are now free from any magic or curse that has been placed on you.*

*You are liberated - forever.*

*Please live the life that you deserve and embrace it fully.*

*Win the alpha challenge next week for me. Although I won't be there to witness your success, from the bottom of my heart, I am happy for you.*

*Remember, I love you. Always.*

*Ivy*

THE WORDS CUT into him like a knife, each one a searing reminder of the sacrifice she had made.

Rage bubbled within him, mingling with the deep sorrow that threatened to tear him apart.

How could she have done this?

"Damn it, Ivy," he growled.

She had negotiated his freedom from the curse that had burdened him for so long, yet she had willingly shackled herself to the underworld in return.

The thought of her trapped there, surrounded by darkness and despair, burned him to the bone.

His heart ached as he thought of Ivy, her beautiful face etched with both love and sadness in their last moments together.

But wallowing in his pain would not bring Ivy back.

He would face the underworld itself if that's what it took to save her soul.

"KNOCK KNOCK!" Ciaran stood at the door.

"It's open, you don't have to knock, and you're halfway inside the room already, Ciaran."

Ciaran shrugged. "Just a precaution. You look like you are about to throw that glass at any moving object, so it would be stupid of me to make sudden noise and startle you."

Ciaran glanced around the room.

"So, Ivy's gone."

"You don't look surprised, Ciaran."

"No, I'm not. I know she made a deal with Selene. She told me when she used her healing magic on me; before you jump, Killian, she only told me because she thought I was totally out of it—it was like a self-confession! So, what did she promise Selene?"

"She said she had sold her soul."

"Hmm…"

"You're not surprised, are you? Did she tell you this during a healing session as well?"

"No. I saw her call Selene when that Alpha Hound was about to rip your throat out. For a goddess like Selene, there's nothing cheap when dealing with her. I guess that's the price Ivy has to pay to save you.

"I'm going to get her back."

"At all costs?"

"Given all she's done for me, yes."

Ciaran shrugged. "All right. Selene wanted an item in our family vault. We got that information when we were in London, remember?"

"Yes. But we bluffed about that one. We don't have a family vault, let alone any treasure in it."

"Well, turns out, we do have a real family vault. I think we're going to get what the goddess wants-- among other things as well. The problem is, if we get to that place, you might not have enough time to go back for your alpha challenge. But there is an astrological lineup when we can open the vault more easily compared to other times."

"Let me guess, that time is now, before the Alpha challenge."

Ciaran nodded. "Are you up for that?"

"Fuck yes."

Ciaran nodded. "Here is the location." Ciaran put an envelope on the table. Killian opened the envelope and pulled out a map. "That's like the end of the world."

"Not quite. But that's a place where we can get up

and down between the underworld and the upperworld-
-like taking an elevator."

This is the end of Wolf Betrayed.

Continue reading **Wolf Turned** - Book 5 of the **Curse of the Alpha** series >> **HERE**

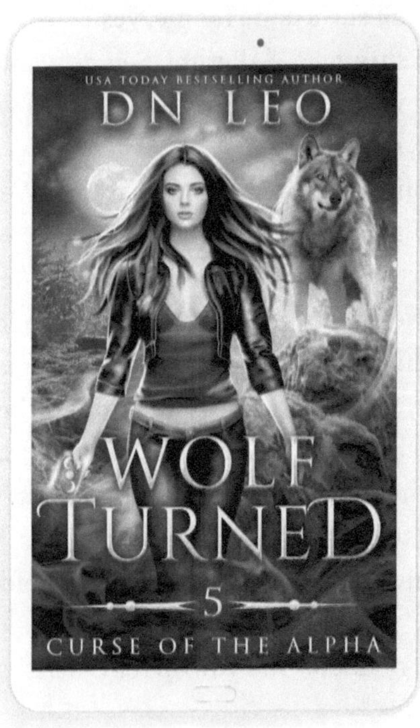

# ALSO BY D.N. LEO

>> D.N. Leo's Master Catalog

**D.N. LEO**

*Building the Multiverse of Happiness*

http://dnleo.com

# AFTERWORD

Thank you for reading.

If you enjoyed reading **Wolf Betrayed**, I would appreciate it if you would help others enjoy this book, too.

**Recommend it.** Please help other readers find this book by recommending it to friends, readers' groups and discussion boards.

**Review it.** Please tell other readers why you liked this book by reviewing it wherever you purchase the book from. If you do write a review, please send me an email at info@dnleo.com so I can thank you with a personal email.

You can find a list of all books I have written at http://dnleo.com